Getting It Twisted

62 Short Stories with No Cohesive Theme

Christopher J. Linzey

P. E. Linzey

A WisdomBuilt® Book

ISBN: 979-8-9863828-7-6

A WisdomBuilt® Book

DEDICATION

This book is dedicated to my family.
I would not be who I am today without all of you in my corner.

CONTENTS

CONTENTS

INTRODUCTION

I have loved stories since I was a kid. In my room at night, I would lie awake and create stories in my head. I was a superhero. I was an adventurer. I was invincible and could do anything and everything I ever wanted. My stories were my chance to see myself as the best version of me. They were my chance to play out scenarios that would never happen in real life.

My love of stories never stopped. It continued into my teen years and manifested in my collection of novels and comic books. I devoured TV shows and movies. While training to be a minister, I even took a class on narrative theology. I LOVE STORIES!

Stories set us apart from every other creature on the planet. No other living thing creates worlds and make-believe people like the narratives humanity enjoys. Through our stories, we experience laughter. Through our stories we process grief. Our stories ground us and elevate us. Our stories make us distinctly human.

When my dad asked if I would like to participate in a "flash fiction writing challenge," I was ecstatic and terrified. Writing one story a day for an entire month? I was ecstatic because I had never put my stories onto the page before. I was terrified for the same reason. But I stuck with it. The stories you have here in this volume are from the twisted brains of me and my dad. Some are humorous. Some are depressing. Some are heart-wrenching. But they are all authentically us.

My desire in sharing these stories with you is that you might find a piece of yourselves in them. I believe we can find a common thread of humor, of nihilism, of humanity, among our shared stories. At the very least, I quite enjoyed partnering with my dad in this endeavor. Every day we would share our stories with each other, and now we share our stories with you. We invite you into our worlds, and hope you can find something that resonates, and hopefully our love of stories is something you can share with us.

Chris

1
A LABOR OF LOVE

"God, I hate gardening. The way my hands feel after working the earth and messing with the plants. The way my back hurts after hours of working. The kind of hurt that doesn't even hit you the day you do your gardening – it's the kind of hurt that doesn't strike until the next day. God, I hate gardening. I don't even know why I do this to myself."

Tom paused in the middle of pulling a weed from the flower bed. In actuality, he did know. It was because of her. After 40 years of marriage, some things just become part of the normal routine – an accepted reality without even thinking about the how's and why's of the thing. And one of the realities of his wife is that she had loved to garden and grow things.

Well, she tried anyway.

What's the opposite of a green thumb? Do we even have an expression for that? Whatever that expression is, that's how Tom would have described his wife.

"Hey, Siri! What's the opposite of a green thumb?"

"The opposite of a green thumb is sometimes called a black thumb."

Ha! That made sense. And that fit his wife to a T. She was a black thumb. She was the queen of black thumbs. Every plant, herb, and flower she had ever brought home ended up withered and dead.

Every. Single. One.

Well, that's not entirely true. There was that one vine plant years ago that ended up growing so much it stretched around the whole living room of their little apartment. It was the first apartment they had after they were married. But then they had moved and that plant somehow didn't make the move with them. So she wasn't a TOTAL black thumb. Maybe just 99.9%.

It's funny the memories that stick with you. That stupid vine that wouldn't die. Everything else, though – toast. Zero chance of survival.

Yet, for all of the floral death that had occurred in their home over the decades, his wife had STILL loved gardening. Tom couldn't understand it. Every couple of weeks there was a new plant or a herb. He could actually watch the thing wither and fade over the weeks. And yet, he knew another would be taking its place before too long.

Tom considered himself an indoor cat. He didn't love nature and the outdoors. Gardening wasn't a pleasure, it was a chore. She would continually be on him about helping out in the garden. Pull weeds. Water the plants. Turn the soil. For the life of him he only ever did it to get her off his back. It was a labor of love, but certainly not love of the garden. It was love for her. He would have done anything for her. And over the decades of their marriage, that "anything" had turned into helping her care for her garden. The garden that would see plants and herbs come and go like a revolving door. Even so, for all of the plants that had come to their untimely end because of her, she never relented in her love of the garden.

That first month after she passed Tom hadn't done anything in the garden. In fact, it looked pretty wretched. But then there was a thought in the back of his head – GO PULL WEEDS! It was the same voice that he had heard for so many decades, a voice that made him roll his eyes. This was her passion – not his.

He ignored it at first.

The thought persisted. GO PULL WEEDS! So he put on his grubby clothes and went out to tend the garden. He did it the next day, too. And the day after that. Without even meaning to, it became part of his regular routine. He didn't have a green thumb, but he certainly wasn't a black thumb. She would have been proud.

Every weekend became about tending to the garden. Her garden.

Their garden.

"God, I hate gardening," Tom thought.

"God, I loved her."

2
THE MONUMENT

For fourteen years, Sam and Maggie would get home from work, change their clothes, and have a light snack. Then they would spend an hour in the garden. That was their haven, their one place where they could be fruitful and at peace.

A long time ago, they thought they would have children, but no matter what they tried, Maggie never had a child. Well, she did get pregnant once, but a painful and traumatic miscarriage ended the dream and with it, her hope of having a family. That's when she asked Sam to build a fence around the backyard so she would have a place to hide, and he did. Her fence was pretty, providing solitude as well as facilitating vining plants, and had a gate in the center of the back section of the fence.

At first, she just sat there. On the ground. Staring. Feeling nothing. Every day after work. Sometimes, even when it was raining. Then she asked Sam if he would get her a bench, or maybe build her one, and he did. For several months, she sat on the bench instead of the ground.

At the supermarket one day, she saw packets of seeds: flowers, vegetables, herbs, bushes. Without much thought, she picked up a packet and placed it into the cart. She had never gardened before and knew nothing about it, but that didn't matter. It was as if an internal force was compelling her towards an unknown future, as if she couldn't help but wade into it and go with the current, and she did.

At the start of the second year of the garden, Sam started noticing the produce on the table at dinnertime. That's when he, for the first time, went out to examine her garden. He saw the rows, the soil, the growth, all the result of Maggie's efforts. There was a good feeling inside of Sam that he didn't have a word for. That's when he started joining her every day after work. For fourteen years, Sam was beside her in the garden.

Their love life had come to an abrupt end with the miscarriage, but they still loved each other. They just didn't know how to process the heartbreak. The garden provided a place for that to happen. Slowly, but certainly.

That's where they talked. That's where they laughed. In fact, that was the only place they had a conversation the entire fourteen years. And as far as either of them could remember, the only place where they laughed.

They were in the garden when the tornado struck. There was no siren in their town. No warning whatsoever. One minute it was calm, and everything was right in their little world within the confines of their fenced-in garden. The next minute contained the fury of an angry sky, as if outside forces could no longer tolerate the serenity of their tiny spot on the planet.

When Sam came to, the wind and the noise had stopped. There was no fence. There was no garden. There was no Maggie. Her body was never found. All that remained in the backyard was the gate, standing all by itself as a monument.

3

OUT TO PASTURE

Bill hated the idea of a retirement home. It flew in the face of every principle he held dear in life as a former sheriff's deputy: freedom, independence, spontaneity, adventure. Retirement homes were not the place for any of these. Here he could only envision imprisonment, dependency, tedium, and boredom. The more he thought about it, the more he hated it. But his daughter hadn't given him a choice. At 78 years old, he was having a harder time moving around, and the independence he so greatly valued was simply not in the cards. His daughter, Stephanie, had a family of her own and she and her kids lived a couple states away. They had talked briefly about the idea of Bill moving in with Steph and the kids, but Bill quickly vetoed that idea. He hated the idea of a retirement home, but he absolutely LOATHED the idea of being a burden on others. He had made his own way in this world, and he would not rely on his extended family for care.

Then last week came the accident. Bill was trying to carry groceries into the house and he slipped on the icy walk. He caught himself on the ground and even managed to save the eggs...but he broke his wrist and twisted an ankle in the process. Maybe Steph was right. Maybe he did need to be in a place that provided additional care. So, begrudgingly, he let Steph check him into Friendly Hills Retirement Residence. Friendly Hills?!? What was he a cow? It reinforced the feeling that his daughter was putting him out to pasture. "Friendly Hills, my ass," he muttered under his breath.

Ugh. The cheeriness nauseated him.

"Hi, William! I'm Jerry, the supervisory nurse for the day shift here at Friendly Hills! We're so glad to have you with us!"

"Bill. It's Bill. Only my mother and my cousin ever called me William." This was already starting off on the wrong foot.

"Okay! Bill it is! Let me wheel you around and make some introductions." Jerry grabbed the handles of Bill's wheelchair and, before Bill could even respond, began pushing him down the hall. "Down here at the end of the hall is the dining room. The meal schedule is on the nightstand in your room. Make sure you try the special dessert on Wednesdays! They change it up every week but it's ALWAYS a real treat!" Jerry kept pushing and talking. In fact, Bill felt as though Jerry never stopped talking. They walked through every space Jerry could think of; every place Bill had zero desire to see. He just wanted to get into his room and mope. Yup, that was it. Bill realized he wasn't above it. He wanted to mope and wallow in his misery for a bit. But cheery Jerry wouldn't stop.

"And here we have our rec room! Make sure you take advantage of all the weekly activities that go on here."

That's when Bill saw something strange. In the corner of the rec room, a resident in leather slippers and still wearing his bathrobe (C'mon, man, it's 3 in the afternoon!) was passing a manila envelope to another man Bill could only assume was another resident. The two men looked around furtively. When they made eye contact with Bill, they whispered in hushed tones and quickly exited out the back door towards the patio. Ever-perky Jerry piped up.

"Oh, those guys! They are so quirky! Once you get to know Theodore and Alby, you'll love them"

Bill wasn't so sure, but he put it out of his mind, determined to be absolutely miserable at Friendly Hills.

That first few weeks were torture. It was everything Bill feared it would be The menu was the same every week: his routine was mind-numbingly routine. He was living in his own personal

Groundhog Day, and it was hell. But then something unexpected happened.

He was in the rec room Tuesday afternoon doing nothing out of the ordinary, but Theodore and Alby were back in that corner he had first seen them in weeks prior. There was another envelope being passed between them. No longer in his wheelchair, Bill had the mobility and the curiosity to poke his nose into other people's business.

"Hey, fellas, what's going on?" Bill tried to sound nonchalant and friendly, but the law enforcement background came out a little too strong and he sounded suspicious and accusatory. "Crap," Bill thought to himself. "Gotta work on that."

Theodore and Alby looked a little nervous. "Nothing going on here," replied Theodore. "We haven't actually interacted much since you checked in. I'm Theo. This is Alby."

Bill wasn't ready to let this go. "Guys, I'll be honest, this is the second time I've seen you handing off manila envelopes. I'm not making accusations, but something feels off."

Alby smiled at him. "Once a LEO, always a LEO, huh?" Alby used the abbreviation for Law Enforcement Officer, which Bill picked up on immediately.

"Does it show?" asked Bill.

"Mostly to those of us who have been in the game," said Alby. "I'm Alby, retired from the Cincinnati P.D. about 15 years ago."

"Nice to meet you," said Bill. "Still doesn't answer my question."

Theo and Alby looked at each other. Then they looked back at Bill. "I think he'd be a fit, Theo," Alby said quietly.

"Your call," said Theo. "It's your show." Alby went on to explain to Bill that the residents of the Friendly Hills Retirement Residence only looked like they were retired. In truth, Alby was the leader of a private detective agency he ran out of the home, and most of the residents were on his staff! The mobile residents were his field agents. The residents with limited 8obilety ran admin and logistics for the detective agency.

"We're the best undercover operation in the state!" Alby said,

8

beaming with pride. "The real secret is that no one expects folks of our age to be much a threat. We're old. We're slow. We're no longer in our prime. That means people underestimate us. You'd be surprised how candid people are in their conversation when they're around old people. They gossip with each other. They share secrets with each other. No one thinks us old guys are a potential risk or threat."

Bill couldn't help but laugh at this. "This is possibly one of the best things I've ever heard in my life," Bill said. "You use people's low expectations against them."

"Absolutely correct," smiled Alby. "Theo has been working a case and the manila folders are case files for our clients. Which brings us to you. Now you know our secret. This isn't a secret society, so I won't pretend to threaten you into silence. We're retirees, not supervillains. But we're always looking for good people to join the team. Whaddya say? Feel like putting some of your past experience to work? it beats waiting every day to see what flavor the Jello of the week is going to be."

Bill stuck out his hand. "I don't know where this is going to take me, but I've never been one to be afraid of jumping into something new. Let's DO this!"

With a smile and a wink, Alby shook his hand. "Welcome to the agency"

4

YOU NEVER KNOW

After the symphony came to a crescendo and the program concluded, the visiting violin soloist took a bow, received her bouquet of roses, and approached the microphone.

"Thank you, ladies and gentlemen. Thank you so much for your kindness. Thank you for being here tonight. It is an honor to accompany your symphony orchestra for this performance. And one more thing. I want to thank Ms. Alberta Carter for being here. Today is Ms. Alberta's one hundredth birthday. Happy birthday, Alberta!"

The audience broke into another round of applause, and as they headed towards the exits, a reporter approached Ms. Carter.

"Ms. Carter, may I ask a question or two?"

"Certainly. What do you want to know?"

"I am covering this event on behalf of the local television station. How do you know Samantha, the guest violinist?"

"Do you mind if I sit down to tell you the story?"

"Not at all. In fact, I will sit down, too. If you don't mind."

"How do I know Samantha?"

- - - - - - - - - -

Every Sunday afternoon, seven students from downtown Alexandria's *River's Edge School of Music* arrived at 1:45 to set up for their music session at the *George Washington Center for the Aged*, otherwise known as "the old folks home." Nobody knew for sure when the retirement home was built. The building itself was so run down that the musicians joked it had probably been there since George Washington himself was an old man.

They had been coming every Sunday, rain or shine, since the music school was formed in 1997. Of course, the members of the group changed every year as some graduated from the program and new students enrolled. But the woman in charge of community service at the school always made sure there were seven musicians ready to play and talk and smile every Sunday afternoon.

The combo always had at least one guitarist, pianist, and drummer. And depending on the participants in a given year, the instruments might include a flute or clarinet, a trumpet or trombone, and in good years, a violin and cello.

The residents enjoyed their Sunday afternoon concerts. They liked seeing the young people. They loved having something to alleviate the boredom. They craved the human connection to the outside world. But what meant the most to them was the affection offered by the instrumentalists.

"The Kids" would smile and talk with them. They often offered a hug or a pat on the back, and being touched by someone other than a medical professional was rare these days. Whenever the topic of conversation got around to family, the consensus among the residents was that after the first year in the home, most of their relatives and friends stopped visiting. All they had to look forward to were the weekly worship service led by the community church, the sabbath service conducted by the local synagogue, and the music program.

"Who's that? A new violinist?" ninety-one-year-old Margaret asked eighty-nine-year-old Alberta.

"I think so," Alberta replied. "I haven't seen her before."

"She looks too young to be at the music school, doesn't she?"

"They get younger every year, Margaret."

"You're right about that!"

"But she looks so sad." Alberta made this observation softly, and Margaret didn't make out all the words.

"What did you say?"

"I said she looks so sad."

"Oh dear. You're right about that, too!"

"Margaret, do you have any note paper with you?"

"No, dear. But I can ask the receptionist if he does."

Margaret excused herself from the program and shuffled out of the room and down the hall to the entrance of the facility.

"Young man? Might you be able to loan me some paper?"

"Of course, Ms. Margaret. How much would you like?"

"Oh, perhaps two sheets, an envelope, and a pen? Would that be all right?"

"Yes ma'am. Here you go."

After the receptionist handed her the stationery from the *George Washington Center for the Aged*, and included the pen and envelope, Margaret made her way back to the music room and sat down next to her friend.

"What are you going to do, Alberta?"

"I want to write her a note and invite her to come visit us sometime, if she ever wants to talk. Who knows? She might want to."

"That's a lovely idea. You never know."

Alberta wrote the note, included her own name and room number, and asked one of the nurses if she would hand it to the young violinist after the next song.

"Of course, Ms. Alberta. I'd be happy to do that for you. But you know our policies. I'll have to open it and read it first."

"I know. That's why I didn't seal it."

The nurse read the note, sealed it, and after the next song, she walked over and gave it to the young girl. She looked at the envelope, then up at the nurse, who pointed over to where Alberta and Margaret were sitting. Alberta waved and smiled.

When the concert was over, the musicians packed up their instruments and took about thirty minutes to talk with the residents. The violinist approached Alberta.

"Hello. My name is Samantha."

As Alberta started to introduce herself and her friend to Samantha, the young girl started to cry, then turned and ran down the hall, her violin in one hand, the envelope in the other.

Four days later, before Alberta started getting ready for supper, there was a knock on her door.

"Ms. Alberta?" knock, knock, knock. "Ms. Alberta?" knock, knock, knock. "You have a visitor." The nurse shouted to make sure she was heard.

Alberta opened the door and immediately recognized Samantha.

"Come in! Come in! I am so glad to see you!"

"Hello. My name is Samantha."

"Yes, I remember, Samantha."

"I was so surprised when the nurse handed me your note last Sunday. You see, I am brand new to the music school, and I wasn't expecting that."

"That was the first time I have written a note to one of the student musicians. But I saw you and noticed three things about you. One, you are a very good violinist. Two, you are very pretty. And three, you seemed so sad. I hope you don't mind my saying so. I don't mean to offend you."

"No, not at all, Ms. Alberta. I was hoping that nobody would notice how sad I was, but I do need someone to talk with, and after reading your note and seeing you wave to me, I wondered if . . ."

"What is it, Samantha?"

"I wondered if I could come and visit you once in a while."

"I would like that."

"I come from a small town, not far from here. A week after I was accepted into the music school, my family died in a car crash. Hit by a drunk driver. My mom and dad and little brother were on their way to my last high school concert. They never got there."

Alberta reached out and placed a hand on Samantha's wrist. Samantha stopped talking long enough to shed a few tears, wipe her eyes, and then continue.

"My parents almost always sat in the same place. But I just

13

assumed they got there a little late and had to sit farther back. I didn't find out what happened to them until after the program ended."

"Oh, Samantha. I'm so sorry."

"I have no other family. Nobody who wants me, anyway. My grandparents are dead. My aunt doesn't have time for me. Or interest, for that matter. And when I read your note, well, for the past few days, I wondered if you might be willing to be my family. I'm not asking for money or anything. I just, I just need someone I can talk to once in a while."

"Samantha, I would be delighted to be your family. It would be an honor."

For the next four years, Samantha visited Alberta once a week, in addition to participating in the Sunday events, and they became quite close. After Samantha graduated and turned professional, Alberta followed her career, sending her a card or flowers from time to time. And whenever Samantha returned to the area, she visited Alberta at the *George Washington Center for the Aged*.

- - - - - - - - - -

"Wait a minute!" the reporter gasped. "Are you Alberta Carter who used to be first violinist of this very symphony?"

"Yes, I am," the centenarian replied. "More importantly, Samantha and I are family."

5
PROOF POSITIVE

Jackson couldn't believe his luck. After years of hunting he finally had it. He had endured all of the ridicule and mocking. He had endured through the personal doubt. He had been a true believer, come to the brink of giving up the faith, but had ultimately remained faithful and come back stronger than ever.

It had been easy being involved in the cryptozoology world. His passion as a photographer and documentarian was to let the world know (and hopefully find photographic or videographic proof) of the creatures he relentlessly pursued.

Bigfoot.

Nessie.

The Chupacabra.

The Jersey Devil.

While others laughed at his desire to capture these magnificent creatures on film, he just KNEW that one day, if he remained steadfast, he would eventually be able to find the proof he so desperately wanted to find.

And now he had it!

He had spent the better part of a month roughing it in the Pacific Northwest. It was, after all, the area in the U.S. that had the highest concentration of Bigfoot sightings. He had learned how to prepare wild fish he caught in the river. He had learned and became comfortable with digging "cat holes" in the forest so he could defecate without disturbing nature. The last month had not been easy, to say the least, but now it was TOTALLY worth it!

He ran out of the forest like a man possessed. His legs were jelly and his lungs were on fire. He must have sprinted a mile and a half before he made it to his truck. It was exactly where he had parked it a month ago, sitting in the parking lot off of State Route 1. Jackson slammed the key into the ignition and the engine roared to life. He HAD to get these pictures to the editor of the Journal of Scientific Exploration. He had been laughed out of the office the last time he was there, but now that he had proof positive they would HAVE to publish his work and tell his story.

This was the vindication he had been waiting for a lifetime to find.

He made it back to his apartment in an unbelievable 24 minutes and ran up the two flights of stairs. Jackson threw open his door and ran to his computer, ready to put the SD memory card into the computer and email the editor he had approached those many months ago. He sat down on his computer chair, booted up his computer, and looked down at his camera.

All of his life had led to this. It was his time.

The computer finished booting up, and Jackson opened the memory card slot on his digital camera.

The slot was empty…

6
BUG #9

As a fourth-year science major with dreams of becoming an entomologist, Enrique loved being at the university. But truth be known, at the start of his last semester, he was more interested in a specific female homo sapiens whom he had encountered than any lepidopteran, hymenopteran, or orthopteran that he had studied, and when it came time to do his senior project, he was smitten. He couldn't focus when reading the textbooks, he daydreamed in his classes, and although he was usually self-disciplined in planning his assignments, he was way behind on this one, and very close to failing the course.

The only problem was that she felt the same way about him, which made his head spin just thinking about her, thinking about them as a couple, thinking about the way he felt when he was with her, and thinking about the future of their life together. They had known each other seven weeks, and already knew they were right for each other.

"Enrique, you have to get it together and finish your senior project. You know my father is against us getting married until we both finish college. And if you don't pass that project, you won't graduate, right?"

"I know it, Cammie. But I'm having trouble keeping my mind on school work. All I can think about is you."

"I'm flattered, Riqué. Really. But what do I have to do to get you to understand that I want to get married just as much as you. That's why I am focused, disciplined, and staying on target with my assignments. And you have to do the same thing or it's not going to work."

"Okay, okay. I'll try harder. Jeez, Cammie!"

"What is your project, anyway?"

"I'm supposed to find an unusual species of an insect, photograph it, and do a write-up."

"Is that hard?"

"How am I supposed to find a rare insect around here?"

"You don't think your professor would assign you something that was impossible, do you?"

"Well, it looks like he did."

"Let me see the assignment."

"Oh, all right."

"It says you're supposed to select something from this list, spend ten hours looking for it in one of these specific locations, and if you don't find one after ten hours, then you can write the report based on research rather than on one that you saw yourself."

"What? Where does it say that?"

"You haven't even read to the end of the instructions, have you?"

"Do I have to answer that?"

"Tell you what, Riqué, next weekend, let's go to the forest or one of the nature trails on the list, and see what we can find."

"You mean, you'll help me?

"No, silly. You have to do the work, but I will go with you."

"Okay. I'll do it."

"Pick a bug, any bug," Cammie suggested playfully.

"I'll take bug number nine."

"Perfect. Bug number nine can be found in three different locations within a hundred miles from the university. You have to decide where you're going to look, get your camera and any other stuff you need, and pick me up Saturday morning at six. I'll pack lunch for us."

Saturday morning, he arrived at her apartment right on time.

She came to the car carrying a basket with their lunch, and they took off. Two hours later, they arrived at the state park and started hunting. Enrique had printed two pictures of Bug #9 so they would know what they were looking for.

They walked and talked. They hunted and searched. By noon, they hadn't seen anything that resembled Bug #9 so they found a place by a stream and ate lunch.

"What if we don't ever find it, Cammie?"

"Then you know what you have to do."

"What?"

"If you don't see it here, then you're spending all day tomorrow in the library doing the research."

"Me? You make it sound like you won't be there with me."

"That's right, Riqué. I'm spending tomorrow with my family. My brother has a soccer game after Mass, and my dad asked me to be there for the game and then dinner."

"And I wasn't invited?"

"I told them you had a tough assignment and you'd be hanging out at the library all day."

"Wow! Thanks!" Enrique was sarcastic, not grateful.

"You're welcome!"

After they had been in the forest for ten hours without seeing Bug #9, it was time to pack up and leave.

"Hey, do you want to get a hamburger or something on the way home, Cammie?"

"Sure. You pick something. Anything'll be fine."

"Okay. Since I picked Bug #9, let's go to the ninth restaurant we come across on the way back. What do you think?"

"Sounds like a fun way to decide where to have dinner. You drive; I'll count."

"Gotta deal."

Enrique made his way back to the entrance of the state park, got onto the freeway, and stepped on the gas. Cammie was on the lookout for places to eat.

Wendy's, Hardee's, Subway.

Longhorn, Charlie's Grill & Pub, Pizza Hut.

Sam's Salad Bar, Olive Garden, La Casita.

That's number nine: La Casita Mexican Restaurant.

It was almost dark when Enrique parked the car. He got out to open Cammie's door when, suddenly, he heard her scream inside the car. He looked in and saw her pointing at the windshield while continuing to scream.

"What are you screaming about, Cammie?"

"Look! Look! Look!"

Enrique looked at the windshield. Right in front of Cammie, a beautiful adult Bug #9 had landed.

"Hand me the camera, Cammie! Quick!"

He took lots of pictures. About half of them were awesome, and he deleted the others.

Then they went inside to eat.

"Now I get to be with you and your family tomorrow." Enrique sounded triumphant as he prepared to take a bite of his burrito.

"No, silly. You're spending the day at the library to finish your project.

"Jeez!"

7
A PIECE OF FICTION

Jason didn't know how he had ended up in the job, but he didn't really care. It felt as though he had the best job in the industry. I mean, it was getting harder and harder for writers to find work in this day and age. His parents had outright pleaded with him to change his college major. His siblings mocked him mercilessly. Who in their right mind, they would ask, would think that a degree in creative writing would get him anywhere these days? How did he even plan to support himself?

Sure, it wasn't easy at first. He had solid grades throughout his university experience. He had even graduated from Emory University, a school with a solid reputation for having a terrific creative writing program.

Still, life after college hadn't been a piece of cake. It was certainly embarrassing asking to move back in with his parents while he was job hunting. Then there was working as a customer service representative while simultaneously trying to land a job writing. He would work his shift while writing stories in his head. Day after day he would practice his craft, working on his tales. His favorite kinds of stories involved conspiracy theories, taking unlikely things and working out nefarious plans to show how they were brought to pass by the powers that be. There's always someone pulling the strings. No big narrative exists in a vacuum. That's why conspiracy theories work so well – everyone knows there's an element of truth, that people with power control the outcomes of the world. So why not write stories about it?

After submitting several pieces to magazines, nothing had ever "popped" for him. Until that one day near the end of last summer.

"Jason Mckay?"

"Yeees?" He answered slowly.

"I represent Commissioner Roger Goodell from the National Football League. We were passed a couple of your stories by an editor who is a friend of the Commissioner. Bottom line up front, we need your help."

"Um…what can I do for you?" Jason wasn't sure where this was going, but he was intrigued. Almost any job would be better than where he was right now.

"We need you to write for the NFL. But before we go any further we're going to need you to sign an NDA."

Jason was now fully intrigued. He had nothing to lose at this point.

"Okay, send the form, I'll sign." Jason had no idea what he was getting into, but a job writing for the NFL? How could he pass the offer?

So he signed the nondisclosure agreement and they flew him out to the NFL headquarters in New York City. And it was there that he got to write the biggest story of his life, about a pop superstar falling in love with a superstar tight end on a winning team that was looking to build a dynasty. Against all odds, the team, arguably one of the worst "best teams in the league," makes it to the big game. It was actually one of the most fanciful storylines he had ever come up with. Surely writing fiction for the NFL was a once-in-a-lifetime kind of opportunity. He really did have the best job in the world. But he wasn't sure how long he could keep this job.

I mean, who on earth could believe such a piece of fiction like that?

8

DREAMS AND PREMONITIONS

When the alarm went off, Mark squinted at the screen to see the time. It felt like the middle of the night, but the digital readout said 6:30. Lori was already out of bed, and he could hear her getting breakfast ready in the kitchen, as well as the familiar, welcome sounds made by the Keurig she got him last Christmas. At times, he wasn't sure who she got that machine for: him or herself. On the other hand, he wasn't sure which he loved more: her or her coffee.

"How long have you been up, Lori?"

"I had a disturbing dream again."

"Sorry to hear that. What was it about?"

"Mark, do you believe in omens? Premonitions? Things like that?"

"I don't know. Never really thought much about it. Why?"

"I had another dream where something happened to my mom."

"Another? I don't think you mentioned that."

"Yeah, for the past week or so. Not every night, but maybe like four or five different dreams about Mom getting hurt, or she's missing, or her house burns down. One of 'em was good. She won something like ten million dollars in the lottery."

"I wish that one came true." Mark laughed.

"Yeah, right."

"When was the last time you talked to you mom?"

"Last weekend."

"Last weekend?"

"Yeah, we always talk on Saturdays."

"And the dreams started when?"

"Sunday, come to think of it."

Mark walked up behind his wife, put his arms around her, and kissed her neck.

"I love you, Lori."

"Love you, too."

He refilled his mug and grabbed the remote.

"I'm surprised you don't have the news channel on."

"I didn't want to wake you up."

"That's kind of you. Thanks."

"Hey, did you know there was in earthquake out in California last night? What town does your mom live in?"

"She's in Westlake Village, near Thousand Oaks."

Lori joined him in the living room just as a reporter came on the screen.

"And now this breaking story, reporting live from Westlake Village near Thousand Oaks, California. The 7.9 earthquake happened last night just after midnight, shaking homes and businesses throughout the community. You can see the devastation behind me. Windows broken, walls of buildings cracked. A fire started in this residential community when a gas line ruptured and then exploded. The fire destroyed more than a dozen homes in this condominium complex. And as the fire burned, a mudslide that authorities believe was caused by the massive earthquake came down that mountain right behind the homes and crashed into the condos. Rescue teams are searching for people in the chaos and the rubble. One woman was found in her living room, buried in mud, a winning lottery ticket in her hand. Of course, names will be withheld until next of kin can be notified."

9

THE WORST PURCHASE

Jackie's mom was not like other mothers. Mothers were supposed to be kind. Mothers were supposed to be nurturing. Mothers were supposed to be the ones you could turn to when life around you was turning to crap and you had nowhere else to go. Jackie's mom had never been that way. For Jackie's mom, nothing was ever good enough. Jackie was never good enough. No matter her grades, she was never smart enough. No matter where she placed on the track team, she was never fast enough. No matter how she did her hair, she was never pretty enough. The theme of Jackie's relationship with her mother could be summed up as "never enough." And still, even after an entire childhood of living like this, and now being on her own for a few years, Jackie still lived under the shadow of her mother's criticism. The only thing that was flawless to Jackie's mom was Louboutin shoes. God, her mother loved those shoes. She never even owned a pair, but she loved them still. The red sole was her dream status symbol.

Jackie had never heard of a sinking fund before, but as soon as she learned about it, she knew it was the ticket to realizing her dream of owning a pair of genuine Louboutin pointed red-sole pumps. Of course she didn't love the shoes herself. She had always preferred comfort over high fashion, and, though her friends teased her for them, her favorite pair of footwear was her baby blue Crocs. No, she didn't love the Louboutin shoes. Her mother had been

25

talking about the brand forever. It was one of the few things her mother seemed enchanted with. Jackie had told herself that getting a pair of shoes like that would finally be the ticket to getting her mother to look at her with dignity and respect. The only problem was the cost. The $845 price tag for a pair of shoes was beyond the pale and she just couldn't find a way to justify the purchase.

Then a few months back while listening to a podcast on money management, she learned about sinking funds. In essence, it's setting money aside every month in your own "fund." As you contribute to it more and more, the fund gets "heavier" and sinks lower and lower until you finally hit your target. Then you can go make your large purchase in cash and not have any debt to pay off. It seemed like a good idea to her!

So she started setting aside $70 every month. It wasn't easy to take $70 away from other things in her budget, but she made it work. Little by little, her sinking fund began to grow.

$70

$140

$210

Soon a full year had come and gone and she had $840 in an envelope whose only purpose was to get her that pair of shoes and, by extension, her mother's respect. So, full of hope in the prospect of finally having her mother compliment her, she drove to the store and bought herself the fanciest and most costly pair of shoes she ever owned.

Now…when and where to wear them?

She had it! There was an upscale restaurant downtown where the company she worked for was hosting a party next week. Everyone in her department had been invited, and it was supposed to be semi-formal. The company was even bringing in a PR team to take official photos of the event to highlight the team and the incredible year they had. It was the PERFECT opportunity to wear the pumps. She could send her mom some high-quality professional pictures. It was settled.

The night of the party finally arrived. The week of waiting was excruciating, but tonight was her time to shine. She had never been so meticulous in doing her hair and makeup. Everything had to be perfect. Not a smudge. Not a hair out of place. Nothing would come up short tonight. Tonight she would be enough. Everything in perfect order to perfectly complement the perfect pair complement

Perfect.

As the cab pulled up to the restaurant, her heart began beating wildly. She could just imagine the looks on her colleagues' faces when they saw her in her shoes. The lights on the restaurant marquee were simply dazzling. The night was magical. Nothing could take this moment from her. Nothing except the sidewalk grate she didn't see because she was so bedazzled by the magic of the night.

The left heel of her brand-new shoes caught in the grate and snapped off with a loud CRRRRAACK! She went tumbling down, dropping her clutch as she desperately reached out to catch herself. The clutch hit the grate and popped open, and she watched, horrified in slow motion, as her keys bounced out of that little purse and through the grate into the darkened sewer below. All she could hear was the sound of her mother's voice in her head saying, "Why didn't you get a purse that zipped up? Why weren't you watching where you were walking? Why did you think you even had a chance of pulling off that look with those shoes?"

Those stupid shoes…

10
THE IDIOT

"Mr. Peterson, my name is Tom Rainier, your court-appointed attorney."

"I told them I don't want a lawyer, so you can pack up your things and . . ."

"Mr. Peterson, listen to me." The lawyer interrupted because he could tell when someone was angry and not paying attention to reason. "Whether you want me here is not the issue. There are two reasons I am here. Number one, the judge appointed me, which is tantamount to him ordering me to be here, so I have to do it. Number two, you need me. I understand you don't want me. I get that. But you do need me."

"I said get out!"

"Let me tell you straight to your face. You are an idiot."

"So, let me see if I'm getting the big picture here. You're my lawyer whether I like it or not, and you're here to tell me I'm an idiot. Did I get that right?"

"Yes, you are correct."

"All right, then, Mr. Fancy Lawyer. Why am I an idiot?"

"I will tell you, but first, let me ask you a few questions."

"Okay. Why not."

"Would it be okay with you for us to use first names instead of the more formal Mr. Me and Mr. You?"

"What do you mean?"

"My name is Tom and yours is Fred. So why don't we leave the formalities for the courtroom and the paperwork, and be real people and friends when it's just the two of us in the room? I'm not here to fight with you or get into an argument."

"You're not here to fight or to argue? That must mean your whole reason for coming was to call me an idiot?"

"Well, my real reason for being here is to help you, but I am willing to do whatever it takes to do that. If calling you an idiot is what it takes to get your attention, then, yes, I will tell you that you are an idiot. On the other hand, it does seem to me that the way you handled yourself in this case is something only an idiot would do, so if the shoe fits . . ." The attorney didn't finish the sentence. Instead, he stopped talking and stared at the inmate.

Fred looked at the lawyer, sized him up, and realized that he really did seem to be a pretty decent guy.

"I'm okay with that."

"You're okay with my calling you an idiot?"

"No! With using first names!"

The lawyer held out his hand and started the meeting all over again.

"Good morning, Fred. My name is Tom, your court-appointed attorney, and I'd like to get you out of jail so you can go home to your wife and kids and get back to work."

"Hi, Tom. Nice to meet you."

After shaking hands, they both started laughing like old friends who just heard the funniest joke ever, and after they settled down, the lawyer proceeded with the interview.

"Fred, can you tell me what happened?"

"Yeah, I needed a set of tires for my truck, so I went over to the tire store and bought four new tires, not the cheap ones, either. Within a week, the tread came off two of 'em, and I realized they cheated me. I paid for top quality tires, and they gave me retreads. Bad ones, at that."

"Then what did you do?"

"I went back to the service center and demanded my money back, or a new set of tires, and they said no. The guy said I needed to look at the fine print in the invoice. There's nothing I can do."

"Okay . . ."

"So, I took them to small claims court. I was mad when I got there. I must have said something wrong, or had a bad attitude, because the judge cited me for contempt of court and threw me in jail, saying I needed a lawyer before he would allow me to proceed with the complaint. Look, Tom, I don't want trouble. I just want some tires so I can get on with my life!"

Fred was getting mad all over again.

"How long have you been in the jail, Fred?"

"Three days."

"Three days! What'd you do? Punch the guy at the tire store?

"No! Well, almost. I threatened him but nothing more."

"Has it been rough in here?"

"Ha! Do you really wanna know?"

"Yes, I do." Tom seemed to be sincere.

"Well, my first night here, I was jumped by three guys who said *If you're gonna live in our house, you need to know who's boss.*"

"Were you hurt very badly?"

"Ha! Are you kidding? They didn't know who they were messing with. I'm a black belt in BJJ, and by the time I took care of 'em, all three were runnin' for cover. If I were to make this my permanent home, which I don't plan to do, I think I would be the boss! Ha!"

"So you're here for threatening the guy at the tire store and yelling in court. And your first day here, you get into a fight with three guys. Is that right?"

"Again, not my fault. C'mon, Tom. Help me out of this mess."

"Okay, Fred. As your lawyer, I have to ask: were they hurt very badly?"

"No, not really. Bruised, sore, aching. Probably wounded pride and humiliation. They didn't need medical attention, if that's what you mean."

"Was the incident reported?"

"Huh. Come to think of it, I don't think so. I didn't. And I doubt that they did. I haven't heard anything from the guards."

"Okay, maybe there's no record of it, then."

"Everyone in here knows about it, though. You would be amazed at the change in the way they all treat me now."

"Fred. I need to see the invoice and any paperwork related to the purchase of those tires. Do you have a copy of it here?"

"Can my wife email it to you?"

"Sure. I already have a copy of the judge's decision to put you in jail."

"Do you think you can get me out?"

"One hundred percent certain of it, Fred. Have your wife send me the invoice, and I'll be back at nine in the morning to set you free."

At exactly nine a.m. the cell door opened, and Fred was a free man. He met Tom in the lobby and thanked him.

"Your court date is in six weeks. Can you stay out of trouble that long?"

"Yeah, I can. What about the tires, Tom?"

"Well, I think I can take care of that. I read the fine print, and I'm pretty sure you have a solid case. We'll take care of that after you rejoin your family and go back to work."

"So, Mr. Fancy Lawyer, do you still think I'm an idiot?"

Tom just smiled.

11

EULOGY FOR A GNOME

Brothers and sisters,

Today we gather to celebrate a life that was taken from this world long before its time. Today we remember Frederick, my beloved garden gnome. Frederick began his journey in this world about a decade ago in the mysterious land we call Taiwan. He was an old soul, and even when he was young still had the appearance of age and wisdom.

From his inauspicious beginnings overseas, Frederick the Garden Gnome immigrated to the United States, coming to this country with hundreds of his kiln kin, where he eventually made it to the shelves of the Home Depot Garden Center.

I remember the first time I ever saw Frederick. He was just standing there, smiling and waving at me. At first, I wasn't sure I was the one he was looking at. I looked around and realized there was no one else near me in the aisle, so he must have been waving at me. Little did I realize that he was just a friendly fellow, for he waved at literally everyone. Still, I knew that I wanted him in my life – and so I took him home with me.

It took my family a little while to get used to the idea of me and Frederick. My wife wasn't happy at all. She became upset and even called Frederick horrible names – names like "Ugly Little Troll" and "Creepy." I would let nothing phase me. Frederick was here to stay. With the kids in the house, though, there was no room for him, and my wife insisted Frederick sleep outside. The nerve!

Frederick didn't complain. He never complained. That's just the way he was. He kept watch over our front yard all those years and never said a negative word. He didn't really talk much, just stood there watching and waving.

I'll be honest, we probably could have gone on like that for years more, if it hadn't been for Mrs. Landry's Great Dane. That dog had no business being off the leash! That big, clumsy oaf. He had gone running after a squirrel and chased the dastardly rodent into our yard and knocked over poor Frederick. He took a nasty tumble over and over and over again – down the little hill in the front yard he went. Had he lungs he would have let out a blood-curling scream. Alas, poor Frederick was forced to suffer in silence, until at long last he came to a stop, head separated from the rest of his body. The sharp edges around his neck where the head snapped off stuck in the soft grass, leaving Frederick's feet sticking straight up in the air. What an undignified way to go.

Oh, Frederick! You were taken too soon! Farewell, dear friend. Farewell.

THE WORLD YOU KNEW

After thirty-seven months exploring the solar system, the four-person team of astronauts finally got the green light to return to Earth. One was from China, one from Spain, one from Ukraine, and one from the United States. Now they were coming home, scheduled to enter Earth's atmosphere in two days, thirteen hours, and six minutes.

The mission had been successful by everyone's metrics, and they had accomplished just about everything they were sent to do. The biggest downside was the time away from their families and friends. Birthdays, anniversaries, and weddings they had missed. Not being there to watch their children's ball games, recitals, and school events.

They didn't get much news while they were gone. "We want you to be able to focus on your task and your mission, so we'll keep the news of world events and politics from reaching you," the mission director had told them. "We'll allow your families to send a weekly message, but we'll scrub them of anything we consider inappropriate. And, of course, you'll be able to reply once a week. Same rules apply."

In addition to the scientific research, one of the aims of the mission planners was to see how people from four diverse nations interacted. They were asked to talk about their homeland, their government, and their culture. They were to talk freely about family values, faith, and taboos. One assignment was to teach each other the basics of their language.

The team handled this part of the mission quite well. They got along amazingly well, and there were few arguments. Each of the four felt enriched by the three-year project. Not only had they contributed significantly to humanity's understanding of outer space, the solar system in particular, they also felt like some major barriers to international relations had been removed.

The four of them had reached a point of talking openly about some of their biases, and managed to get beyond them. They hoped to share that part of the journey after returning to Earth, and came up with a plan to write, give public talks, and share privately with friends. They even wanted to approach their nations' governments, schools, and business organizations. The broader the coverage and exposure, they reasoned, the greater the possibility mankind could finally overcome its problems with international relations and interpersonal hate.

The closer they got to the end of their time in space, the more their families talked about being there when they landed. The parties, ceremonies, and celebrations they would have. And they were all starting to get excited. The landing would be at a small NASA-owned location in Central Alaska in June, each government making sure the family members were there in time.

The four astronauts even talked from time to time about how they would be perceived by their friends, neighbors, and communities. They tried to remain humble, but they did feel a sense of pride, and expected to be treated like national and international heroes.

"Hey, do you really think there will be some parades and TV talk shows?" they wondered.

They hit the atmosphere at not quite the best angle, and instead of entering, they bounced off.

"That's OK, team," they heard on the communication system. "It was a mild deflection. You'll orbit the Earth three times and then reposition yourselves to enter the atmosphere. Just a delay of a few hours."

After the third orbit, they successfully entered Earth's upper atmosphere and started their descent. They could feel the temperature rise, but the heat shield did its job, and it wasn't long before they were on the ground. They opened the hatch and stepped out triumphantly.

"Where is the crowd?"

"Where are our families?"

"This is eerie?"

"Not what I expected."

"Nobody's here."

One of them let down a ladder so they could climb down to the ground. The nearest hangar was about a quarter of a mile back, but as they were walking in that direction, they saw a van heading towards them. The driver was a woman in a Canadian Air Force uniform. She stopped the van and got out.

"Welcome home!" she shouted, trying to sound as cheerful as possible.

"Where is everyone? We were told our families would be here, representatives from our countries."

"You haven't heard?"

"We haven't heard any news the past three years."

"The world is at war. Your families are not here. There's chaos and fighting in Europe, Africa, North and South America, Asia, and Australia. The world that you knew three years ago is dead."

The four friends looked at each other and climbed into the van, each of them wondering what lay in store for them, for their family, for their world.

13
WAR OF THE WORDS

Most families have their squabbles. Some families have feuds. Occasionally, families go to war against each other. This was the case with Victor and Gregory. The sad part is that these combative siblings were once the closest of friends.

Growing up they were always by each other's sides. Nearly inseparable, only 17 months apart in age, they always had each other. No matter what was happening in the world, Victor knew that Gregory would always have his back. They went through their formative years this way. Born in the early 1400's, surviving childhood was, in and of itself, no small feat. But then adulthood came, and with it came the inevitable change that always accompanies leaving childhood behind.

Their father, a semi-educated man, had taken great pains to make sure the boys had received as much education as possible. Admittedly, he could only take them so far, and 15th century Europe was a hard life for the uneducated and unattached person. But like the saying goes, it's not what you know but who you know that matters. Victor and Gregory's father had made connections with wealthy and educated people through his import business and arranged for the boys to become apprentices. Sadly, the apprenticeships meant that the boys would finally have to separate.

Victor became an apprentice to Peter Schoffer, a Parisian scribe. Gregory went to apprentice with Johan Fust, a merchant and bookseller. And that is when their worlds collided.

It's funny to think about the little things in life that divide us. Sometimes it's not the obvious divisions that hurt the most, but the little things that get under our skin and end up causing a big rift. Such was the case of Victor and Gregory, as their apprenticeships brought them into the sphere of Johannes Gutenberg. Shofer and Fust both agreed to partner with Gutenberg to develop a newfangled contraption – a metal press that put letters onto paper. Victor and Gregory, as mere apprentices, were tasked with the hard work of research and development.

Victor immediately fell in love with serif font-types. Those decorative lines on the ends of the letters were so delicate and beautiful. They transformed letters from mere means of communication into art itself. How could anyone want anything other than serif fonts?

But Gregory never found that kind of love. With a personality more austere and matter-of-fact, Gregory believed serif fonts to be silly and wasteful. How could anyone deny the simple, functional glory of a sans serif font? And thus two brothers, raised as best friends, began a font war that would last their lifetime and carry on for generations to come.

"Serif fonts are more attractive!"

"Sans serif fonts are easy on the eyes!"

And while our two brothers are long dead and gone, their war continues to this day. Without even realizing it, you have been already been recruited to one side or the other.

14

THE SALISBURY FONT

"The note said, *Read the Salisbury Font.* That's all. Nothing more. Just, *Read the Salisbury Font.*"

"So, what did you do?"

"I got online and typed *Salisbury Font* and discovered there are more than a dozen graphic arts companies that designed a font called *Salisbury*, and they're all different."

"I understand what it would mean if it said to write with a certain font, but to read a font? That doesn't make sense."

"I know. That's what I don't get. We have to figure it out today, though, or we're in trouble. Our appointment is at seven o'clock tonight, and if we don't have it when we get there, we might be out of luck. This may be our only chance to prove we didn't do it."

"Show me the note."

Geoffery handed it to Emily.

"It says *the Salisbury Font.* Is it implying there's only one?"

"Hmmm. I hadn't considered that."

"And *Font* is capitalized."

"And that means?"

"Usually, a word is capitalized at the start of a sentence."

"Or if it's a title or a name."

"Exactly. So, what is *the Salisbury Font*?"

"Emily, Salisbury Cathedral has a world-famous baptismal font. I've never been there, but I've heard about it."

"Okay, assuming that's what this refers to, how would someone *read* a font?"

"I don't know, but we have to find out. We're running out of time."

Geoffery and Emily had worked at the Secret Intelligence Service, commonly called MI6, for the past ten years. Two years ago, they were assigned to work together. And one month ago, they were accused of stealing state secrets and selling them to foreign governments, and possibly involved in an assassination plot. It was a serious charge. They were being framed, but they had no proof. How can you prove that you didn't do something? They didn't want to hide any longer, so they had made arrangements to turn themselves in.

Geoffery looked at his watch. It was 1:30 in the afternoon.

"Salisbury is about two hours from here. Let's go see what it says."

"I'll drive. I go faster," Emily reminded him.

When they got to the cathedral in Salisbury, there were a handful of tourists outside the main entrance. Inside, they were greeted by a docent.

"Welcome to the Cathedral."

"Thanks. We're here to see the font."

"Beautiful. I hope you'll make your way back to the Magna Carta, too. In fact, there's quite a lot to see here. A lot of history."

"Thank you so much. We'll do that."

The desperate spies approached the font and were impressed by its size and by the reflection of the stained-glass windows in the water.

"Geoffery, Look!"

Emily had noticed that there was an inscription on each side of the font.

"The note says to *Read the Salisbury font*. This is it!"

Side One: *Do not fear for I have redeemed you.*

Side Two: *I have called you by name, you are mine.*

Side Three: *When you pass through the waters, I will be with you.*

Side Four: *And through the rivers, they shall not overwhelm you.*

"Okay, now what do we do?"

"There's got to be a clue in what it says."

They read all four inscriptions again. Then again.

"*When you pass through the waters,*" Geoffery read aloud. "*And through the rivers.* Emily, maybe we're supposed to go *through the waters.* Maybe there's something hidden in the water."

He glanced over at the docent, who was looking the other direction while helping another visitor.

"I have to find out!"

Geoffery rolled up a sleeve and put his hand in the water. At first, it was shallow, but as his hand moved farther from the edges, it was deeper than he expected. Then his fingers hit up against something that moved. Something small, flat, and round. It felt like a metal coin or medallion, perhaps two inches in diameter, much like the challenge coins given by the military when a soldier was to be honored for something he had done.

"Hurry! She's coming!" Emily said.

Geoffery picked up the coin, put it in his pocket, and they ran out. As they returned to the car, he dried his hand and wrist, rolled down his sleeve, and pulled out the coin. There was a name and address etched on the back.

"Do you recognize it?" Emily asked.

"I have no idea who that is. It's a Yorkshire address, though, which means we don't have time to check it out. I would suggest that we return to HQ, turn ourselves in, show them the medallion, and hope for the best.

"You mean . . . trust the very people who think we're guilty?" Emily wasn't sure that was a good idea.

"Yes. That's what I mean. We did nothing wrong. We have nothing to hide. And I, for one, don't want to spend weeks, months, or years incognito somewhere. You don't have to do it, but I am turning myself in."

She started the car and began mulling over her options as she headed towards London.

"We've been partners two years. It's been a great experience. And now it comes down to this?" Emily asked.

"I know. Our fate rests on that coin . . . Maybe."

By the time they arrived at Vauxhall, Emily agreed with Geoffery. They turned in the keys to the car, handed over their guns and ID's, and emptied their pockets, wallet, and purse.

"What's this medallion?" the agent processing them asked.

"That's what we found today. Trying to find a clue to something that might clear our names, we got a tip that led us to that. We don't know what it means, but that's all we have."

They followed the agent down the hall and were placed in different rooms, pending a transfer to a prison the next day. In the morning, after a fitful night with little sleep, they were escorted to their boss's office.

"Do you two have any idea what the etching on that coin means?"

"No, sir," They replied.

"Two of our people went to that address last night. We've been looking for the man named on the coin for the past year. He gave us information about a terrorist plot to assassinate the Prime Minister, and he provided names and locations. He also told us that the two of you were innocent and gave our guys the names of the people who were responsible. We expect to have them in custody within the hour."

"You mean . . ."

"It means you are exonerated. And I apologize for the accusations against you. Take a week or so off. Spend time with friends or family. And come back to work ready for your next assignment."

Emily and Geoffery looked at each other, then back at their boss.

"By the way, where did you find the coin?" he asked.

15

I HAVE A NAME

I have a name. My mother gave it to me.

Anila.

My mother is Indian and named me after one of the gods of the elements. I am the wind. I am the breath that inhabits the world. I am the destructive power that lays to waste when my fury is unleashed.

My mother told me from the day I was born that there was something special, yet wild, within me. That my spirit echoed the pounding drums in our tribal ceremonies. Anila. I have a name.

I also have a speech impediment. From my earliest years, words have been difficult for me to form. And, as hard as it is for me to form my words, it is often harder for people to truly understand them. My father was an American poet and professor. He was an original hippie who never really put much thought or structure into parenting. I was raised on jazz and folk rock but never taught how to behave in "polite society."

As I grew up, my wildness never subsided. I continued to live up to my namesake, and my fury and destructive power came out in powerful bursts. When I came of age, I left my parents' home in search of something I could call my own. I spent too much time on park benches without any real place to stay. I couldn't hold down any real job – my outbursts saw to that. And that's when I found Dr. Teeth.

Or rather I should say that Dr. Teeth found me. Don't let the name fool you – he's not a real doctor. He was a musician, an amazing virtuoso on the keyboard who had an infectious grin that showed all his pearly whites. He claimed he had never had a cavity in all his decades of life. Dr. Teeth. It was a fantastic stage name, though. It intrigued people. As talented as he was on the keys, he never wanted to do anything but play rock music.

Rock was something I understood. My hippie father had wanted me to be a musician, but my wildness made it hard to manipulate an instrument. Until Dr. Teeth put a pair of drumsticks in my hands. It was like a rebirth – a spiritual awakening. I was born for this. The drum kit and I lost all sense of separation. I was the drums. The drums were me. Dr. Teeth gave me my calling.

"This is a narrative of very heavy-duty proportions!"

He was always dramatic like that. Still, I was grateful for him and his invitation to play drums for the band he was putting together.

"Kid, what's your name?"

"Anila."

"What was that?"

My speech impediment reared it head. I tried again. "Anila."

Dr. Teeth looked at me quizzically. "Animal?"

My fury took over. I started waving my arms around and grunting and yelling. "A-ni-la! A-ni-la!"

Dr. Teeth shook his head. "Okay, Animal it is." I sighed with resignation. For the rest of my career I would be stuck – forever known as Animal. The Muppets didn't mean it in a derogatory way. In fact, it did sort of fit with my wild outbursts. My mother knew at my birth what my legacy would be.

I have a name.

Anila.

Animal the Drummer.

16

TROUBLE IN DRY GULCH

Jake rode into town from the east; Bart came in from the west. They didn't know the other would be there.

Slightly less than two hundred feet long, the only street in Dry Gulch had five buildings on one side and five on the other. On the north were a general store, a saloon, a blacksmith, the stables, and Main Street Boarding House and Brothel. On the south were the bank, the telegraph and post office, the jail, and two houses. One house belonged to the doctor, and the other to the sheriff.

Jake tied his horse to the hitching post in front of the saloon, glanced down the row and recognized Bart's horse in front of the general store.

"What's he doing here?" he groused to his horse, who he had named Broot a long time ago. The appellation just seemed to fit, even if Jake couldn't spell it right.

Broot turned his brown-and-white head toward Jake, then looked down the street. He saw Clyde, and immediately wanted to be tied up down there, instead of over here by the saloon. He started whinnying, pawing in the dirt, and fidgeting, hoping Jake would get the hint.

"What's that, ol' Broot? Maybe you do need to see the smithy. It has been a hard ride."

Jake untied the horse and walked him over to the blacksmith. He tied him up next to Bart's horse, and walked inside.

Now, you have to understand something. Most humans have no idea that horses can communicate by using a sophisticated system of ear twitching, tail swishing, shivering, pawing, rearing, fidgeting, and stomping, combined with the grunts, snorts, whinnying, and other assorted sounds known only to equines. In fact, there is evidence that horses and mules were astonished that it took so long historically for humans to develop the Morse Code, the tap code, and other forms of communicating. "Why, we've been doing that for eons," one old mare said to another.

"Hi, Broot. Haven't seen you since you were a pup!"

"Hello, Clyde. Look at you, all grown up. What are you doing in this god-for-saken town?"

"Well, to tell you the truth, Bart's been lookin' for Jake. Plans to shoot him dead, if he ever finds him. But if you're here, then I would assume that Jake is here. Is that right?"

"Yup. In fact, he's been alookin' for Bart to do the same to him."

"You don't suppose there's gonna be trouble in Dry Gulch, do ya?"

"I reckon there is, Clyde."

Now, a horse can hear sounds up to two miles away, and sometimes even farther. So it should come as no surprise that they heard Bart and Jake arguing inside the blacksmith shop.

"Jake, I been looking for you for eleven years to kill you."

"And I been looking to do the same thing to you that same eleven years, Bart."

"Well, I guess this is my lucky day, 'cause here you are, and by sundown you'll be dead."

"Or. Maybe it's my lucky day."

"You wanna step outside an' take care of business now? Or should we bring the horses in first."

"I'd just as soon take care of business."

The two outlaws stepped out into the sunshine and walked past their horses.

"Clyde, what are they doing?"
"Looks bad, Broot. I'm feeling agitated."
"Yeah, me too!
"Let's listen to what those guys are saying and see what happens"?
"And hope we don't get shot! You've seen things go awry in situations like these, haven't you?"
"I certainly have!"

The gunmen positioned themselves opposite each other.
"Anything you wanna say before you die, Bart?"
"Just one thing, Bart. How's your Pa?"
"He's fine. How's your Ma?"
"I told you not to talk about my Ma."
"So, you're ready to do this?"
"I'm ready."

"Uh oh, Broot. It's happening!"
"I see it, Clyde, but I never thought it would come to this."

The two men stared at each other. The sun blazed overhead. A number of people stood in front of the saloon, the boarding house, and the general store.

Suddenly, Jake drew his weapon and fired. Bart was a split second behind in pulling his pistol out of the holster, but he was faster, and he fired at the same time. Both men fell to the ground.

The doctor ran over to take a look, as the people moved slowly towards the two men lying in the dirt. The doctor got up, faced the crowd, and said, "Looks like the Bannister brothers killed each other."

The End

"Tell us another story, Uncle Broot."

"Naw, that's enough for right now, Colt. You and Filly run along and play. I need to talk with your dad for a while."

"Okay."

"The kids love hearing about when we were young, Broot. And you're a great story teller."

"Thanks, Clyde. Boy, it's good to be in the same pasture as you agin!"

17
BONA FIDE PRODIGY

Every synapse in his young brain was firing. He was in the zone. He had never heard of the concept of flow before, but if he had he would have realized that he had achieved flow. His consciousness was perfectly aligned with his body. Every movement connected in synchronicity with his artistic vision.

He was alone in his laboratory. He preferred it this way. Other people were mere distractions from his genius, and distractions meant mistakes. He couldn't afford any mistakes. This must be perfect, just the way he saw it in his mind's eye. Nine years old wasn't too young to be called a...called a....

What was the word grandma used? Protégé? No, that wasn't it.

Prodigy! That's it. He was a bona fide prodigy, and he aimed to prove it to the rest of the world. Well, at least to the rest of the family. And so he furiously set about his work.

Hot water. We must have foundation of hot water. Three gallons ought to do the trick. Once the water was in place, he knew instinctively what came next. Three handfuls...hands-ful? Shoot. He wasn't sure which one it was. He should have been paying better attention when Mrs. Webster was teaching language arts. Whatever! Mrs. Webster could wait. He settled on handfuls – three of them – of eucalyptus leaves harvested from the tree in his family's backyard. The leaves slowly became saturated with the hot water. Now for the twigs! He hadn't measured the twigs, but he knew how many felt right, and what felt right was two "bunches" of twigs. His base was coming together nicely. But making it palatable required something special.

He held up the cup of 2% milk he had snuck from the refrigerator when Mom was distracted helping his older brother with some schoolwork. With the care of a surgeon, he deftly poured the cup of milk from front to back. The milk added a ghastly tone to the bathtub filled with water, leaves, and twigs. Finally, the pepper! He was too short to reach Mom's fresh cracked pepper. He had to settle for the cheap stuff from the table salt and pepper shaker. These people had NO CLUE the sacrifices he had to make in his pursuit of excellence.

Once the concoction was complete, he began to stir with a fervor that would have made Macbeth's witches proud. The bathtub came to life with this unholy mixture, but he could not have been more proud. After a full minute of stirring, he had finished his masterpiece. It was finished. His heart bursting with pride he exploded from the bathroom and called the others.

"Mom! Dad! COME SEE MY CREATION!!!"

9

DADDY'S WORLD

"Does it work?"

"We're about to find out, Molly."

She was tired of hearing Freddie talk about his wonderful ideas, because they never resulted in anything that actually worked. Thirty-one years of this nonsense, without a single patent. His great ideas were never more than make believe fantasies. He worked full-time in his basement workshop, they had three kids, and she's the one who supported the family the entire time. Thirty-one years of this. She had long ago run out of hope.

The basement was like his haven, his heaven, his playground, and probably much like the inside of his head: full, cluttered, and useless. Several times she had told him, "You'll probably die down there and nobody will miss you."

Molly wanted to tell him that this was the last failure she would endure. If it didn't work this time, he should realize it was never going to happen, and that it was time to rejoin the real world.

All Freddy heard was, "yip-yip-yip-yip-yip-yip-yip-yip, mum-mum-mum-mum-mum-mum, get a job!"

The kids were grown and had productive careers. When they were young, they loved playing in "Daddy's World," which is what they called the basement back then and still called it today. Only back then, they said with playful delight. Now, it was sarcastic derision.

Molly had already gone upstairs, unwilling to watch another dud or explosion.

"But this time, it'll be different, Molly!"

"Just don't burn the house down this time, Freddy!"

Freddy dimmed the lights and held his breath. When he flipped the switch, there was no explosion, no fire. Two lights came on, one orange and one green, just like they were supposed to. He could hear a faint humming from the device, just like he expected. He walked over to the far side of the room where the other part of this invention sat on a table. He flipped the switch, and it, too, came alive. Two lights came on, and a digital readout flashed some numbers. Freddy grabbed a stool and sat down. He didn't know what to say. It seemed like it was working.

Forty-three minutes later, Molly opened the basement door.

"Freddy?"

No answer.

"Freddy? You still down there?

All was quiet.

She tip-toed down the stairs and saw Freddy lying on the floor with a smile on his face. His eyes were open. There was no pulse.

19

PEACE IS OVERRATED

A year.

One. Full. Year.

Three Hundred Sixty-five days.

That had been the longest year of Jimmy's life. To be fair, he had been EXTREMELY lucky to make it into the shelter as the first missiles started falling. Sure, people had laughed at him the entire time he had been building his shelter. They continued to laugh as he painstakingly stocked it with food, water, and other supplies.

"You REALLY think you'll ever need that?!?" That was the most common jeer. Of course he did! You don't take the time, trouble, and finances to build a fallout shelter just on a whim. He had seen the signs of the times. Jimmy knew it was eventually coming down to the end of things as they knew it. What was it the computer called it in that old movie? That one with Matthew Broderick and the AI? Oh, yeah – GLOBAL THERMONUCLEAR WAR. They had tried to tell us through the movies decades ago. But people get complacent. People think things will be okay. People forget the real threat of villains in the world. Not Jimmy. He never forgot. Thus the shelter went from dream, to plans on paper, to a reality.

Then the bombs arrived.

By chance he happened to be a few minutes from the shelter when he heard the news report. D.C. first. Then New York. Then

L.A. That was as far as he heard before he made it inside and sealed the shelter off from the rest of the world. The first couple of days were the easiest. He was still amped up and was committed to the cause. He had his planned routine from waking to sleeping. But then the days turned into weeks, and boredom was not just a concept but a reality that gnawed at his soul. He lived in his very own Groundhog Day, each day being a bleak repetition of the one before. He hadn't brought enough books and read each one multiple times. At least he had enough food and water, but food and water didn't help his state-of-mind and mental health.

The one year anniversary actually came as a relief. Radiation levels should be down enough to allow him to venture out for days before the need to return to the shelter. That was more than enough time to find new supplies. He needed to restock. He cracked open the seal of the shelter and ever so slowly opened the hatch. Everything SEEMED normal. Since his shelter was away from any main road, he didn't really expect to see anything yet anyway. He arranged his camouflage netting over his shelter to hide it from a quick glance. If someone was determined enough to search they would eventually see it, but it could fool a cursory look.

Then he set off.

After an hour of walking, he had found several stores that still had some canned goods. He had enough to fill his backpack. He wasn't worried about his nutrition. The concerning thing that he couldn't shake was the bodies.

So many bodies.

Everywhere he went, the dead were ever present. The putrid smell of decay was something that would be forever seared into his memory. So many bodies, but no people. Not living, anyway. One hour stretched into two, and two into three. Still no signs of life. He was all alone. They had actually done it – destroyed humanity. As far he could tell, he was all alone. He laughed to himself. "All those years complaining about noise, population, the city…now I can finally have peace!" Three hours turned into three days, into three weeks, into three years.

Peace is overrated.

20
KEEP YOUR COOL

Joan was angry, hurt, and disappointed, though it was hard to say which she felt more. She was sure the promotion would be hers. Instead, it went to Frank. She knew he was a good guy. After all, she had hired and trained him. She even liked him. She knew he could do the job. That wasn't the point. What she couldn't understand was why he would be selected for this position instead of her, in effect, making him her supervisor. Was it because he was a man? She hadn't considered that until now because there had never been any indication that the leadership in the company was sexist.

Two weeks had passed: two weeks of mulling it over, tossing and turning every night, and working through the issues and emotions. She had gone through all the steps of grieving, had come to accept the decision, and even arrived at a pretty good attitude. Perhaps she'd get another chance someday.

One morning, she got an email from her boss, asking her to meet him in his office at 11:30. "I wonder what he wants." At 11:15, she reread the email, looking for a hint of a clue as to what he might have in mind. Then she walked down the hall to face the music.

"Joan," her boss said. "I need to talk with you about why the board of directors selected Frank instead of you."

"Look, Thomas. Before you say anything, I admit that I was upset about not being selected for the position. But I've come to peace with it. You don't have to worry about me being a problem. I can handle it and continue to be a positive force on your team."

"That's what I like and respect about you, Joan. In addition to being smart and talented, you are strong. You don't let circumstances knock you off balance. You keep your cool, even when things look bad. In fact, the board of directors feels the same. That's why I asked to talk with you. You see, there were two leadership positions we needed to fill. We put Frank into one of them. The other is a vice president position."

"We have two vice presidents: you and Henry. Are you talking about yours or Henry's position?"

"Henry decided to retire, but for personal reasons, he didn't want to announce it until today. That's why I couldn't tell you before now. We are offering you the VP role instead of the job you applied for. And it includes a much more significant increase in salary."

"I didn't know Henry was considering retirement. Is he okay, Thomas?"

"Since you are now my peer, I can tell you. Henry's wife has stage four cancer, and he wants to step away so he can spend as much time with her as possible."

"I didn't know."

"None of us knew. So, what do you say? I think you are perfect for the job."

"Thank you for letting me know. I accept."

"I'm glad to hear that, Joan. I told the board that you would. There's a press conference at noon to make the announcement, followed by a luncheon with the board of directors. Are you hungry?"

21
#MOMLIFE

5:00 a.m. – Middle child had a nightmare and woke up screaming. Went in and comforted and rocked him until he rolled back into a restless sleep. Now back to bed to squeeze out a few more minutes for myself.

6:00 a.m. – Up for real this time. Make a cup of coffee. Knock on the kids' doors to get them up for school.

6:30 a.m. – Coffee gone. Time to make school lunches. Wake the kids up AGAIN. Some screaming through closed doors, something like, "I'M UP! LEAVE ME ALONE!" Teenagers, pfft.

7:00 a.m. – Kids are out the door to catch the bus. I don't think they dressed with enough layers for the temperature today, but that was not a fight worth having. Look at this mess they left behind in the kitchen. Every. Single. Day. Sigh – time to get to work.

7:45 a.m. – Kitchen cleaned up. One day they'll appreciate me. One day. Time for some self-care.

8:45 a.m. – 3 mile bike ride and morning yoga complete.

9:00 a.m. – Showered. Feel refreshed. Feel...human...again.

9:30 a.m. – School board meeting. I'm pretty sure most of this stuff could have been handled in an email, but here we are.

11:00 a.m. – Coffee connection with Sarah! It's nice to have a moment to talk with another adult without any agenda to drive the conversation.

1:00 p.m. – Pick up the oldest from school for his doctor's

appointment. Hopefully we can figure out what that pain in his stomach has been about.

2:30 p.m. – Back to the house to make sure there's a parent at the house when the bus drops off the middle schoolers. Time to play enforcer and see that homework gets done.

4:30 p.m. – Dinner prep. What are we eating tonight? Oh, crap! What are we eating tonight? What do we even have in the pantry? How about the freezer? Okay, frozen burritos and salad it is.

6:00 p.m. – Clean the kitchen post-dinner. I swear, this room is cleaned more than the entire house and yet it never seems to be done.

6:30 p.m. – Bathtime. Please get in the shower. No, I don't care WHO went first last night – I asked you to go shower right now. You know what? I don't care if you want to switch, but you have to ask your sibling. If they say no, you just gotta obey.

8:00 p.m. – Kids are clean. Finally. Now if I can get them to floss and brush their teeth.

8:30 p.m. – All the kids are in bed and lights out! Victory!

8:45 p.m. – All the kids are in bed and lights out. I hope?

9:00 p.m. – GET IN BED! KEEP THE LIGHT OFF!

9:15 p.m. – Crash on the couch. Husband wants to watch a show. I can give him maybe 20 minutes before Cinderella's coach turns into a pumpkin.

9:30..

22
ALONE

When the alarm blasted him into the realm of the living, he jumped out of bed and got started, hoping that the kids weren't awake, yet, because his tasks were invariably faster and easier when he was alone.

Alone. He remembered those days. Back then, he hated being alone. He wanted a wife and kids. Then he got married. Then they had kids. Now he'd give anything to have one day all to himself. Just one day. Was that too much to ask?

Jack and Millie had been married thirteen years. Their kids were eleven, nine, six, and five. The first two were girls, followed by two boys.

He packed four lunch boxes. He got breakfast ready and on the table. He made himself a cup of coffee and his wife a cup of her favorite tea. He woke up the kids and helped them dress for school. He helped Millie get out of bed, use the bathroom, wash up, and get into the wheelchair. He kissed her and rolled her down the hall and into the kitchen so the family could be together for breakfast.

When everyone had eaten, each child hugged and kissed their mom before he drove them to school. He returned to help Millie get settled for the day, waited for the caregiver to arrive, then went to work.

Fortunately, he liked his job and had been there long enough to have earned the respect of his boss and co-workers. They all understood what he had been going through ever since the collision that put him and the kids in the hospital and made his wife a quadriplegic. He typically put in a four-hour shift at the office and was allowed to work from home the rest of the day. That concession was because the insurance plan provided a caregiver only three hours per day, meaning Millie would only have to be alone for about an hour each day.

They had no family in the area. Most of their friends had been helpful at the start. Unfortunately, they ran out of availability or interest because they stopped visiting, calling, and helping after the third month. He understood, but still felt abandoned and alone.

After picking up the kids from school, his evening routine kicked in: preparing dinner, cleaning up the kitchen, supervising homework, putting on a video for the kids while he provided personal care for Millie. Then after baths: assembling the family in the living room for Story Time with Mom.

Millie had been a schoolteacher and Sunday school teacher and loved to read to the kids. Jack got a small table to put the book on, and the kids took turns holding the book open and turning pages for her.

Story time with Mom was Jack's only down time. He sat on the sofa, usually one or two children on his lap. Most nights he'd fall asleep to the sound of her voice.

23
HIGHLY DISTURBING

"COME OUT WITH YOUR HANDS UP!"

Tony was REALLY confused. He heard a voice on a loudspeaker but didn't know where it was coming from.

"COME OUT WITH YOUR HANDS UP!"

It seemed like the voice was really close. Like – SUPER close. He moseyed over to the window to take a look outside. WHAT THE...?!?! His house was surrounded by dozens of police. He even saw what looked like a S.W.A.T. tank. Holy crap.

"COME OUT WITH YOUR HANDS UP!"

There was the voice again. He finally spotted a fifty-something looking man in a light blue button-down shirt under a tactical flak jacket who was holding a bullhorn. That must be the dude talking. Tony was simultaneously excited, scared, and bewildered. He was only 17 years old and had never had any run-ins with law enforcement before. Never. His mom was an elementary school teacher, and his dad was the sales manager at the RV dealership across town. He was fairly certain that his parents were two of the most clean-cut people on the face of the earth.

"IF YOU DON'T SURRENDER YOURSELF IN THE NEXT FIVE MINUTES, WE WILL STORM THE HOUSE!" The dude sounded serious. He cautiously opened the door, making sure to keep his hands visible at all times.

"Good afternoon, officers. Is...is there something I can help with? My parents aren't home, just me and my little brother." Tony had been doing homework while his 14 year old brother was just messing around online, not really doing anything productive. The man in the blue shirt approached him. Tony could see the lettering on his tactical vest read DHS – department of homeland security. The man lowered the megaphone and spoke directly to Tony.

"Young man, you're in a world of trouble. We were sent here by the Secret Service in response to a highly disturbing Google search that took place just 30 minutes ago." Tony paled when he heard this. He hadn't been online. His homework tonight was a worksheet from his Spanish class.

"TYLER!!!!"

Tony's younger brother popped his head out around the corner of the hallway that led to their bedrooms.

"Hey, man, what's up?" Tyler was not easily impressed by authority or by his bigger brother.

"WHAT ON EARTH HAVE YOU BEEN GOOGLING?!?!?"

24
TAKE A RISK

The composition class was tomorrow morning at eight, and Professor Claredon needed a video. He loved teaching. He loved his students. He loved coming up with creative ideas to encourage and inspire them in ways that helped them succeed. Their assignment was to write a five-page paper on what it meant to take a risk, a leap of faith, and how doing so can lead to success.

He didn't have anything in his files, so he looked online. To his delight, the possibilities were endless. Now he just had to watch videos until he found the right one.

"Aha! There it is!"

The professor copied the link and pasted it into his lesson plan. Then he had a cuppa tea and went to bed.

In class the next morning, he welcomed the students and introduced the assignment. The video he had selected showed two hang gliders at Yosemite National Park. They got out of the pickup truck, put on their gear, and strapped themselves into the kites. Then they walked over to the edge of the cliff, three thousand feet above the valley floor, stood there for a minute or two, and jumped.

After a split-second of freefall, the wind filled the fabric and the kites began to soar. The exhilarating flight over the beautiful valley below lasted more than an hour. Fortunately, the video itself lasted only five minutes, and Professor Claredon asked the students if they had any questions. One hand went up from a kid named Jake in the back of the room. Halfway into the semester, Jake had never willingly participated in class discussion. But now, something had finally inspired him.

"Yes, Jake. You have a question?"

"Yeah. Have you ever seen the Red Bull video about the guy who jumped from a rocket and skydived down to Earth? He actually broke the sound barrier on his way down!"

"I saw that," Teresa shouted.

"Me too!" Several others got excited because they had seen it.

"Can we see that one?" Jake asked.

Having students participate in class discussions is every teacher's dream, so of course, the professor went along with it. By now, he wanted to see it, too.

"How do I find it, Jake?"

"Easy. Just google *Red Bull space jump*."

The video came up immediately, and Professor Claredon watched it with the class. The discussion about stepping out and taking a risk took on a whole new dimension after that. And when the students turned in their assignment a few days later, the professor realized he had hit a home run.

25

A WORK IN PROGRESS

Priscilla sat and stared at her screen. She didn't flinch. Didn't move a muscle. She sat. And stared. Ugh! This was absolutely ridiculous. She should be much further along by now. In fact, she should be done. Complete. Finito. Wait – was that even a real word? Sure, everyone said it, but was is slang or was it real?

"C'mon, Prissy, you're a writer. You should know this."

She had hated that nickname since she was a kid. Whenever she started to spiral into negative self-talk, she always ended up calling herself that name. Ugh. Fine, let's just look it up and THEN get back to work. Finito. Oh. Apparently, it's Italian for "finished." She had used it correctly. Correct usage always made her feel warm on the inside, even if she was the only one who knew. Okay, back to work!

She had been working on this manuscript for what seemed like an eternity. Her editor certainly had been pestering her every single week asking for updates. This was the price to pay after getting a little success. Her first book had been a surprise hit. Some reviewer on TikTok had made a video about her book and she sold 3,000 copies in the first week of publication, 7,500 by the end of the first month. She had never expected that!

But that was a year ago, and now as a published author with a "best seller" under her belt, the demand to produce more felt heavier than ever. Priscilla was afraid that she had overpromised what she could actually deliver to the publisher. Her mother had tried to console her.

"Rome wasn't built in a day, Sweetheart!"

Priscilla knew her mother was trying to be helpful, but sometimes people with good hearts were not good at consoling people living through stress and anxiety. So she sat at her keyboard day after day, trying to come up with that flash of brilliance that critics said had marked her first book.

Ugh. She did not FEEL brilliant. She felt like a fraud. A phony. A conman. Conwoman? Ugh, more rabbit trails. She would never complete the manuscript this way. Her phone rang. She looked at the caller id. Her publisher. Again. The third time that week. She had let it go to voicemail the last time he called. She supposed it would be rude to do that two times in a row. Suck it up, girlie, and answer the phone.

"Marty! Hey, Priscilla here. What's up?" She hoped her voice sounded cheery and hopeful, because she certainly wasn't feeling that way lately.

"Priscilla, darling! How's the new manuscript coming along?" Marty was always upbeat, with a lilt in her voice that most people found endearing.

"I think this could be even better than the last one!" Priscilla lied. What else was she supposed to do?!?

"So what kind of timeframe are we looking at here?" Marty always refused to leave well enough alone and wanted to push deadlines. Ugh.

"Well, it's a work in progress."

14

TRANS-SPECIES MOLECULAR PROJECTION

Shelly was quite upset that her science project didn't make it to the final round of the competition.

"What do you mean, it won't work? It does!" She confronted her teacher and insisted.

"Shelly, it's not real science. It's a fake. A sham." Her teacher was emphatic.

"Aren't you even going to let me demonstrate it, Ms. Hoffman?"

"No! You're making a mockery of the science fair and all the other students who actually did some scientific research and designed a genuine project."

"So let me get this straight. You're judging me and my project simply because you never heard of Trans-Species Molecular Projection and assume it's a fraud? Is that it?"

"Look Shelly. You can't turn cats into turtles. You can't turn a pig into a hawk. And there's no way you can make a human being become an iguana. It's the dumbest, phoniest thing a student has ever tried to pass off as science, and believe me, I've seen a lot of dumb!"

"Where have you been the past ten years, Ms. Hoffman. Is your head still buried in the sand? You won't even let me show you how it works? All I need is ten minutes and I will prove you are wrong."

"Shelly, pack up your stuff and call you parents to come pick you up. Your grade is an F."

On the night of the regional science fair, the brightest students from every high school in the county had set up their projects and were waiting for a chance to demonstrate what they had learned and the scientific devices they had created. Everyone except Shelly, that is. Students had to have their teacher's approval to enter their work, and Ms. Hoffman was adamant in her refusal. There was no appeal process.

Shelly asked her dad if he would drop her and her friend, Margot, off at the theater for the movie they wanted to see, some science fiction thriller, and he agreed to take them.

"I'll come back for you after the show, Shelly. Just text me when you're ready."

"Okay, Dad. Thanks. Love you."

The theater was only four blocks from the convention center where the science fair was getting ready to start. Shelly and Margot hurried over and set up her TSMP in the balcony, plugged it in, turned it on, aimed it towards the stage, and waited.

The Superintendent of Schools kicked off the meeting with an inspiring welcome, congratulating all the students for the fine work they had done. Then he introduced the three-person committee who planned the event. Mr. Jenson, Mr. Rice, and Ms. Hoffman stood up and waved as the audience applauded. Then they took their seats.

"Ms. Hoffman, would you come to the microphone and explain to everyone the purpose for this event and the planning that went into it?"

Ms. Hoffman suddenly wasn't there.

"Has anyone seen her?" the superintendent asked into the microphone.

Nobody had seen her leave, and nobody was listening to the superintendent. They were distracted and amused by the biggest iguana any of them could imagine, scurrying off the stage, down the steps, and out the side door.

27
ODDBALL

It's easy to pick on the outsider.

The oddball.

The one who talks funny.

It's not my fault I have a thick and heavy accent. Did you realize I speak four languages with amazing fluency? FOUR! And when I'm talking to myself in my head there's no accent – just me. When it comes time to speak out loud in front of you I try REALLY hard to enunciate and get my words to sound right. Sill - every single time…

"I VANT TO SUCK YOUR BLOOD!"

Holy crap. It's those blasted double-u words.

It's hard to be a menacing vampire when people are laughing at your accent.

28
STICKY TRAPS

When the spider came along, I was beside myself.

As a rule, I don't hate insects. In fact, I am fascinated by them, and I love most of them. Ladybugs, butterflies, and grasshoppers are my favorites. When they are on the lawn or in the flowers, I can spend hours looking at them, holding them, talking to them. What's even better is that they talk back to me, and we engage in some rather fascinating conversations. I call them "My Friends."

Yesterday, I mentioned to my friends that I hate spiders.

"Oh, I agree," said one pretty, little ladybug. "They're ugly, they're creepy, they're mean. And what's with that extra pair of legs? I mean, really!"

"What's worse," the Duke of Burgundy replied while resting on the back of my hand, "they put their sticky traps all over the place, and if you get stuck in one, they come along and eatcha!" His wings were trembling at the very thought of being caught in a web.

"I know," the grasshopper lamented. "It happened to my little brother just the other day. Poor kid. I wanted to help him, but there was nothing I could do."

"So be careful, Muff. I know you're bigger than the rest of us, but some of them will even bite people," the ladybug warned.

As my friends walked, flew, or hopped away, I decided to have my morning snack. So I sat on my tuffet, which I'm sure you know is this short, little seat that my father made for me in his workshop.

Soon after I started eating my curds and whey, that's when the spider came along.

I'm glad Miss Ladybug told me about what spiders can do to people. I didn't want one of those ugly, creepy, mean bugs with eight legs to bite me! I was so scared that I ran away as fast as I could.

29

THE SIGN

Mark sat on the edge of his seat. He had always wondered about that expression. How often did people use it metaphorically instead of literally. But his butt was actually at the edge of his seat. He was shaking with excitement and was surprised he could even sit down. Could this be the moment? He had been waiting for the better part of a decade, searching the heavens above and the ancient manuscripts long forgotten. He had consulted with prophets and wise gurus, people who were way more attuned than he. Everything seemed to be pointing to right here, right now.

All he needed was the sign.

Admittedly, the hardest part of waiting and looking for the sign was the fact that he didn't know what the sign would even be. They don't tell you that in the ancient texts. So he watched. He waited. But then he knew. He KNEW.

The amazing thing about the sign was that it wasn't a singular event. No, it was a combination of events – a perfect combination of events that pointed in one singular direction. The meteor. The cataclysm in Asia. The election and the consolidation of power in the West. They had all been hinted at in the text. Mark just never realized they were simultaneous happenings. There was only one piece left to complete the ancient foretelling, and that's what he was waiting for now.

On the edge of his seat.

30
JANEESHA

As a little girl, Janeesha loved riding the city bus to go downtown with her mother, and they would go once a month. They could have taken the car, but Janeesha loved riding the bus, and her mother indulged. There were other things she did with her dad, but he didn't like shopping.

"Naw, you girls go on and have fun. I don't need to go shopping with you."

That was always his reply when Janeesha or Momma asked if he wanted to go with them. Their home was three blocks from the corner where a bus would stop once every hour, so they had to plan it just right. If they missed the bus, they had to wait an hour til the next one.

"Hurry up, girl," her mother would say.

"But Momma, I have to finish tying my shoe."

"All right, honey. But we have to get there on time."

"I know, Momma."

At age four-and-a-half, she learned to tie her shoelaces and loved doing it by herself. She was so proud. As she got older and learned new skills, that was still her attitude. She liked being independent, doing things for herself, and the satisfaction that went with it, whatever it might be.

When she reached school age, she got to ride the school bus every single day. That was special, and the feeling never faded.

When she was in high school, the whole family took a three-day bus trip to visit a national park. Again, they could easily have taken the family car, but her parents both enjoyed catering to their kids' interests, and Janeesha always preferred taking a bus, so they accommodated her. Her little brother and sister merely tolerated her.

Now that she was out of school, she needed a job and had several options. Her love of buses never died, however, and she thought maybe being a driver would be fun. But should she apply to drive for the municipal bus service? Or should she drive a school bus? Or maybe even one of those long-distance bus lines? She had seen an ad for Greyhound and wondered what that might be like, going to new cities and towns across the country.

She clearly remembered her monthly shopping trips with Momma, riding the school bus every day, and that once-in-a-lifetime family trip. But which job would be right for her?

"Well, honey," her mother said, "just follow your heart."

Her dad's approach was a bit more pragmatic.

"You know, Janeesha, there are some key differences you might want to take into account."

"Like what, Dad?"

"Oh, things like how much they pay. What kind of hours you have to work. Days off. And does the job take you away from home long stretches at a time. Things like that."

"Thanks, Dad. I'll check into it."

Apparently, her dad had thought about this a while.

Janeesha signed up at a bus driving school. It was a four-week course for the basic training, with a follow-up advanced course. In the evenings, she investigated the questions her dad had raised.

One Saturday morning when she and her mother walked to the corner for their monthly shopping trip, the bus didn't arrive when they expected it.

"We must have missed it, Momma."

"Maybe so," her mother said.

"Do you want to wait an hour or take the car?"

"Well, we have plans for dinner at your aunt's home," Momma

replied. "Let's go ahead and drive."

As they were getting close to the mall, the traffic was totally gridlocked. Up ahead, they saw several emergency vehicles, lights flashing, and people milling about. Momma parked the car, and Janeesha walked over to find out what had happened. Seeing a police officer at the intersection, she went over to talk with him.

"What's going on?"

"There was a bad collision in the intersection," the policeman said.

"Was that bus involved?" she asked.

"No, not at all." The cop said. "The bus was about a block away when the collision happened. The driver saw it, pulled his bus as close as he could, and called 911. Then he got out and started helping the people in both vehicles. Several were hurt bad. Looks like he saved their lives."

"Really?"

"Yeah. The man obviously has been trained in emergency response, first aid, CPR. I've never seen a city bus driver do that. This guy is a hero. If nobody else does, I plan to nominate him for some sort of hero award. He's amazing!"

"Thanks, officer."

Janeesha went back to her mother, who was waiting at the car.

"Momma, I've decided to be a city bus driver."

31

DISCOVERY

"Doc, how long are we going to keep pushing today? It's HOT!"

Miles struggled to keep up with Doctor Lawrence, the department head of the botany department at the university. Miles could very vaguely remember volunteering for this summer assignment. At the time, it seemed like a lot of fun. When Doc Lawrence had first gathered all his research assistants together to discuss the trip, it truly seemed like an adventure. Spend a couple of months trekking through the jungles of South America in search of a rare flowering plant? Sure! He had to beat out Tracy, that suck up research assistant who was always trying to cozy up to Doc, but he had managed to wrangle the spot.

Why oh why hadn't he let Tracy come instead? Then she could have been the one suffering in this intense jungle heat, trying to keep a sometimes scatterbrained professor on track. Okay, fine – it's not that Doc Lawrence was scatterbrained. It's just that he got so focused on a single thing that the parts of life that normal people thought of were never even a blip on Doc's radar. So Miles did a lot of cat-herding trying to keep the professor on track. They hadn't gotten lost or kidnapped yet, but they were only a month into the journey and had roughly a month to go.

"Doc, how much longer? Doc? PROFESSOR LAWRENCE?!?"

"Hmm? What? Oh, Miles, what were you saying?" Doc Lawrence paused to look behind him at his sweaty and out of breath research assistant.

"How much longer are we going to push today? Maybe we should call it and start fresh in the morning when it's cooler." Miles knew what the answer was going to be before he even asked it. It's what the answer always was. Doc was a single man with no interest outside whatever passion he was currently focused on, so he never even thought about slowing down or taking a break.

"Onward, my young apprentice! ONWARD!" The professor plunged further into the jungle, shouting over his should while he marched on. "You know the perspicuous amazonica flower is the last of its kind, and we cannot ignore the reported sighting. We must find it! The ancients claimed that it could be ground into a fine powder that could cure a variety of ailments and prolong life."

Sigh. Miles had heard all the stories. He knew the legends. And a find like this really could bring a radical shift to the medical profession – even in this modern age. While that brought SOME consolation, Professor Lawrence didn't really care about any of that. He wasn't a bad man. It's not that he didn't care about medical breakthroughs. But he was a scientific purist, a botanist's botanist. He wanted to find what no one else could find. For Doc, it was all about the discovery.

To find the last of a species...

32

TOMORROW

The doctor walked in looking like he hadn't slept in two days, which was probably true.

"Your husband's condition is a lot worse than we thought, Mrs. Johnson. I'm afraid he has a rare condition that can't be treated."

"What do you mean? Why can't you treat it?"

"The tests and his symptoms point to the same thing, a rare form of malaria with only one cure. But because we haven't seen this kind of malaria in over thirty years, the drug used to treat it isn't available."

"Well, can't you get it?"

"No, ma'am. Malaria is caused by parasites in certain mosquitoes, and as far as we know, this particular parasite is found in the female of only one species. We could use the saliva of an infected mosquito, if we had one. The problem is that this species is almost extinct because of pesticides and loss of habitat. It could take weeks or months to locate one."

"What about drugs that simulate the molecular structure? I've read that some medicines and drugs can be created like that."

"You've done your homework, Mrs. Johnson, and you're right. Pharmaceutical scientists have been working to create a drug that would function the same way, but because it is rare, there hasn't been much of a hurry to complete it, and very little time or money has been invested in the project. Progress has been slow. So far, it hasn't proven to be effective, and therefore, hasn't been approved for use."

"Not even on an experimental basis?"

"No, not even on that basis. I'm so sorry."

"But, Doctor, there must be something you can do."

"All we can do is care for him and try to ease the pain and discomfort."

"And watch him die?"

"I'm so sorry, ma'am."

"I want to appeal. What government agency do I have to call?"

"Mrs. Johnson . . ."

"I have to try!"

"An appeal, even if expedited, would take too long. He probably has less than twenty-four hours left."

"You mean, tomorrow?"

33

AN UNLIKELY PAIR

The Great War changed everything. Life that was taken for granted previously was never looked at the same again. Across the globe, people of all nations began to see the darkness around them. Hope faded, and the joy that had been in the world slowly began to fade. It was into this dark time that the United Federation of Foods, the UFF, questioned whether or not they should even hold their decennial council.

Unbeknownst to the majority of the population, every 10 years representatives of the various food groups and types gathered together to chart a course for the coming decade. With the state of the world, would they even convene their esteemed congregation in 1920? Dairy sent a worldwide telegram inviting all parties to the conference. Crackers & Cookies were game. Beef was even on board. The toughest sell was Produce, who was having their own internal strife – a veritable civil war between Fruits & Vegetables. Still, they managed to set aside their differences for the sake of the UFF and world peace. Thus the United Federation of Foods World Council of 1920 convened in a hotel on the outskirts of London.

"Welcome, everyone! We're go glad you're here with us this year!" Dairy tried to be gracious towards all of the conference attendees. The problem was that over half of the world's population had a visceral, physical problem with Dairy.

"Who put her in charge?" Poultry shook his head as he muttered quietly to Fish. "I swear, she wants to be liked SO badly, but it's never gonna happen."

"If everyone would please take your seats, we will begin the conference." Dairy knew how people felt. Didn't they realize that the world was changing? The intolerance of old was being set aside. She felt that this was her big year for a comeback!

"We make a motion that the 20's be declared 'YEAR OF THE COW'!" Beef always began meetings like this. He was so predictable. He had tried for years to work his way into goulash, stroganoff, and stews. There was even the coup of 1880 when he managed to make Chicken Fried Steak a beef dish. What a brouhaha that caused. Poultry really had her feathers ruffled over that one.

"Does anyone second the motion?" Dairy knew no one would, but she had to maintain order and discipline in the meeting. The room was met with total silence. Finally, a small voice in the back spoke up.

"I think, in an effort to reestablish friendship and unity with the UFF, this next decade ought to be a team effort. Let us combine two of us into a partnership the world has never seen before!" This was from Produce, but one of the members the Vegetable Faction.

"I second that motion!" Grain raised his hand to the surprise of everyone. No one in recent history could ever think of a time when Grain willingly went along with a plan from Produce. Maybe the Great War really HAD changed them all.

"Motion carries," said Dairy. "Now then, who among us shall we pair up to unveil to the world?"

Dairy's one simple question led to days of bickering and fighting. No one could agree on the right pairing. Some ideas were so grotesque that the mere thought of them made people retch. Some people had their ideas shot down without even consideration, and this made them very salty.

At last, Nuts & Legumes spoke up.

"We have a new member from our delegation that has only been around for a little while. This is his third UFF conference, so you may not have noticed him. He goes by the name of Peanut Butter."

Dairy bristled when she heard the name. PEANUTS ARE NOT BUTTER. She had fought this fight since Peanut Butter was introduced to the UFF in the 1890s. If she could find an unlikely person to team Peanut Butter with, this could be her chance to get rid of him forever! She spoke up.

"I think Peanut Butter is an excellent candidate to unite with another member to promote to the world!" She flashed her most magnanimous smile. "Who is willing to team up with Peanut Butter for this assignment?"

The Fruit Faction within Produce realized that this was their time to shine. Most of their delegates were sweet and paired nicely with salty. They whispered furiously to their Vegetable Faction counterparts.

"If you let us have this win, we'll give you Tomato." This would be a big win for the Vegetable Faction – getting Tomato on their side?!? They couldn't pass on this opportunity.

"You have a deal!"

The Produce representative stood up. "The Vegetable and Fruit Factions within Produce jointly nominate for this special team assignment...BANANA!"

There were murmurings amongst all the delegates. Peanut Butter and Banana? Was this even possible? How would the world react to it? Dairy smiled to herself. "This is it," she thought. The world could not possibly go for such an unlikely team. Peanut Butter and Banana? Ludicrous."

"So let it be written. So let it be done." The words came out of her mouth and all of the delegates cheered. Some were hopeful. Others were doubtful How could such an unlikely team of a Fruit and a Legume ever grab hold of the world? Would it ever take hold? Dairy didn't think so. Poultry was all a-flutter. Beef felt ignored.

It was touch and go for a few years, until an enterprising publisher made a bold choice and, in 1939, released "The American Woman's Cookbook" with a recipe for a peanut butter and banana sandwich.

The rest, as they say, is history.

34

AN UNEXPECTED WIN

Don loved baseball his entire life. He had been a highly rated infielder in high school, was recruited by a couple of major league teams, and actually played Double-A ball for three seasons. But he peaked at that level and never went farther. After that, he was interested in becoming a coach, but life always seemed to be too busy, and the demands of supporting a family were too urgent, so it never happened. He passed his love of baseball on to his four sons and helped them develop their skills, but because of his job, he was never able to coach.

Last year, he and his wife, Sandy, decided it was time to retire. They took a cruise, drove coast-to-coast a couple of times, and crossed a few other things off their lifetime to-do list. And along the way, that old nagging desire to be a baseball coach resurfaced.

After hearing that the local Little League was seeking to expand, Don asked if he could coach a new team. "Sure," The league director said. "But you need to know that your team will be at a disadvantage the first few years because you'll start with no returning players. You're starting from scratch."

"That's okay," he said. "We'll build from the ground up."

After the league tryouts and player evaluation period came to a close, Don and Sandy made a list of the players they were interested in. Some of the boys on their list were good, but the majority seemed to be young fellas who they felt compassion for. Some seemed to come from a rough background.

"Sandy, what would you think about us building a team of some of these down-on-their-luck boys?"

"Us?"

"Well, you're in this too, aren't you?"

"I'd love to, Coach. If you want me, that is."

"I think it'd be fun to do this together. I mean, I'll be the head coach. But you know the game, too, having lived with me, raising four ballplayers, and all. So, what do you think?"

"I think that would be a good thing to do, but you'll have to keep in mind the interests of the better athletes, too."

"What do you mean?"

"Well, those who are already good will want to win right away. And maybe they won't want to be on, what should we call it? A developmental team."

"I see what you're saying. I wondered about that, myself."

"But if that's what you want to do, you old softie, maybe we should start the season off with a bar-b-que and invite all the families. And explain our plan."

"As a way of getting their buy-in?"

"Yeah."

"That's a great idea. Let's do it."

Of the twelve boys on the team, nine had never played any sport. The other three were pretty good. Don took the three good players out for lunch a day or two before the first team practice and asked if they would be willing to serve as player-coaches.

"You boys are already really good, and I know you want to win. So do I. But if we can teach the new boys the basic skills, and encourage them, maybe we can win a few games, have some fun, and position ourselves to be a really good team next year."

Surprisingly, the three of them responded positively. "Sure, we'll do that, coach," said the best of the three.

The first few games were disasters, and everyone was discouraged, including Don and Sandy. "That's okay, boys. Good effort today. Hold your head high and come to practice ready to learn and improve." Don did his best to remain upbeat.

Sandy filmed the game and made a few notes about how to encourage each of the players. Over the next week, she visited the home of each person on the team and gave personal encouragement, not only to the players, but also to the moms and dads and brothers and sisters. Don's focus was helping the boys on the practice field.

They lost games two and three, but the fourth game was really close, a one-point loss. In the dugout after the game, Sandy announced, "Listen up, team. If we win next week, we're having a pizza party."

"You didn't mention that to me, Sandy," Don said on the way home.

"Are you upset, Coach?"

"No, not at all. I think it's a great idea. Pleasantly surprised, that's all."

The next practice went really well. Don, Sandy, and the three experienced players paired off with the newer boys for some one-on-one coaching and mentoring. When it came time for the next game, spirits were high. Every player had at least one family member in the stands, which had not been the case before, and when they won the game, cheers erupted as family members flooded the field.

One of the boys approached Sandy, off to the side. "Ms. Coach?"

"Yes?"

"Can my sister go with us to the pizza party? We don't have any food at home, and . . ."

"Of course she can come. Why don't you go and ask you parents if they would like to join us, too."

35

A DREAMER

People who looked at Sam never thought there was much there. He never made much of an impression on anyone. He was a quiet guy. In fact, Sam hardly ever spoke out loud. It wasn't that he couldn't speak. He just never really seemed to have anything to say that others cared to hear. He knew how people saw him. Standoffish. Weird. So why speak to them? The nicest person in his life while he was young was Mrs. Jensen, his language arts teacher. He once overheard another student badmouth him in front of Mrs. Jensen. Her only response was to say, "Oh, don't mind Sam. He's a dreamer."

Sam knew he was smart. He had never failed any class all through high school. It wasn't an intelligence issue. He just preferred to spend his time daydreaming. His daydreams were legendary. He was legendary. He was a superhero with unimaginable powers and a driving desire to save the world from the villain. He was suave and sophisticated and won the heart of the beautiful girl. He was funny and well-liked, a popular comedian. He was a valiant knight, attacking the dragon's lair to recover the treasure guarded by that forked-tongue beast.

Every time Sam came out of his reverie, he sighed a heavy sigh as reality set in. He was back. Back in the real world where there were no heroes. He was not courageous. He never got the girl. There was no comeuppance for people who were jerks. In the real world, bad things happened to good people and sometimes the sucky people had fantastic lives where nothing went wrong.

No, Sam preferred to live in his own imagination. It was more pleasant there, and it was always ready for him whenever he wanted to get away. He could even pause the daydream if the real world interrupted with something stupid like housework or his job. Then he could just hit "play" and resume the daydream right where he left off. If the daydream was good enough, sometimes he'd revisit the same one over and over again. If once was good, twice was even better, right?

Mrs. Jensen was right. He WAS a dreamer. It was certainly a better world for him than the one everyone else lived in. Walking into his apartment at the end of the day, he threw his keys in the bowl by the door, tossed his coat over the chair by his little kitchen table, and plopped down on the couch. Sam closed his eyes.

36

POINTLESS

She sat on the narrow windowsill in the kitchen of her fourth-story apartment staring out. One foot was on the floor, one butt-cheek on the sill, one shoulder against the cold window. Her head, slightly tilting towards the outside, was cradled in the corner against the casing and the top rail of the lower window.

Straight ahead, only ten feet away, was the solid brick wall of the neighboring building. Straight up was the sky, but it wasn't visible from her perch because both buildings were too tall. Straight down was supposed to be grass, but instead, there was nothing but dirt, if she didn't count the three car tires, two discarded bicycles, one hundred and sixty-seven beer cans, and the water hose that didn't connect to anything because there wasn't a spigot on that side of the building.

She started counting the bricks in the adjacent building, one day, but stopped when she reached two thousand, because she realized that was pointless, just like her life.[1]

---

[1] This story is based on an oil painting by Jonathan Simon.
https://www.jtsimonfineart.com/fig.htm.

37
SWEET CHEEKS

Rumble rumble rumble rumble.

Ooof. Eddie's stomach did not feel good at all.

Gurgle rumble blorrp.

Blorrp? He had never heard his stomach make THAT sound before. Something was definitely off. He racked his brain, trying to recall what he had eaten in the last 24 hours. Oh please oh please oh please oh please just sit tight until he got home. Hold on, man, just hold on. Eddie was standing in the middle of the supermarket with his wife. To be honest, he hated having to use any toilet that wasn't in his own home. Call him picky, he didn't care. There's something unsavory about planting your sweet cheeks on public porcelain. He felt no shame about preferring his own commode.

But emergencies were emergencies. Eddie grimaced. He didn't think his stomach was going to play nice and way until they got home. It had blorrped at him. His wife shot him a curious look in the bread aisle.

"Are you okay, Dude? I can hear your stomach from two feet away and it sounds ANGRY." She always called him Dude. It had started when they were dating. Fifteen years later and the moniker had stuck. He was Dude. She was Bro. Thinking about it, it wasn't really romantic and it didn't even make much sense, but it worked for them.

"Bro, I think I'm in trouble." Eddie suddenly had a panicked look flash across his face. Without another word he ran to the supermarket restroom. Strange toilet be danged, he couldn't wait another moment. He was lucky enough to get his trousers down and just barely get his bum on the seat when his stomach had finally had enough and let loose.

The smell was fierce. It could have killed small animals and made grown men weep. When his stomach finally settled down, Eddie opened his eyes. He hadn't even realized that his eyes and hands were all clenched through the process. As his vision slowly came into focus, he saw the sign taped to the door of the stall:

TOILET OUT OF ORDER AND DOESN'T FLUSH
PLEASE USE THE OTHER ONE

38

THE INTRUDER

Thirty minutes after her husband left to go to the airport, the doorbell rang. When Jennifer opened the door to see who was there, the intruder wasted no time. Before she even knew what was happening, he pushed his way into the house, knocked her to the ground, pounded her head against the floor several times, started slapping her in the face, and dragged her into the dining room. He tied her hands behind her back and duct-taped her to a chair.

"Where is it?" The intruder demanded.

Dazed and in pain, she asked, "Where is what?"

"The lottery ticket you bought last night."

"I didn't buy a lottery ticket."

He hit her again. "I followed you from the store, so I know it was you. Then the eleven o'clock news announced the winner and showed your picture. It's all over town, so don't lie to me. You have two minutes to give it to me or this will not end well for you."

"I was at the store. The lady in front of me bought several lottery tickets. I don't know how many. But it wasn't me. If someone reported it was me, they made a mistake."

"So, you want to play it that way, eh. I don't believe you."

He walked down the hall to her bedroom, found her purse, and returned to the dining room.

"Okay, let's take a look," he sneered as he dumped the contents of the purse onto the table.

He searched her wallet, each compartment of the purse, her checkbook, and inside the mini package of tissues. He removed the cover from her phone to see if the lottery ticket might be hidden there, and pried open her cosmetic kit just in case she might have stuck it in there. He even looked inside the little tube of lip balm. Still, he could not find what he was looking for. By now, he was in a rage. He slugged her in the jaw and sprayed her in the face with her own can of pepper spray.

"Where is it?"

"I told you. It wasn't me."

Jennifer was in pain. The slaps, the head bashing, the punch in the face, and now the pepper spray. Hell, itself, couldn't be this bad, could it?

The intruder went into the kitchen and dumped the trash onto the floor. He searched the dressers in the bedroom. He went into the living room and scanned the shelves, then the drawers in the kitchen. He went through the pockets of the clothes in the closet. Back in the living room, he looked under the sofa and under the cushions.

"I know it was you," he shouted two inches from her face, and then hit her again.

Jennifer was still tied up and duct-taped to the chair when he left, leaving the front door slightly open. An hour later, her phone rang. It was her husband calling. He left a voice mail saying he had checked in and was at the gate. He'd call when he landed. Two hours after that, her phone rang. A friend from work called to confirm their lunch appointment.

Two hours and fifteen minutes after that, a car pulled into the driveway. Jennifer shuddered when she heard the doorbell ring.

"Jennifer? Are you home?" It was her friend from work.

"Maribel, I'm in the dining room."

"Jennifer!"

Maribel untied her, found some scissors, and cut the duct tape.

"When you didn't answer your phone, didn't show up for work, and didn't show up for lunch, I just knew something was wrong."

"Thank you for coming, Maribel." Jennifer put her arms around her friend and sobbed. "Would you take me to the Urgent Care?"

"Of course."

Jennifer called the police to report the intruder. Two police officers were there within a few minutes, took her statement, and looked around. Jennifer put all the stuff back into her purse, locked the front door, and got into her friend's car. On the way to Urgent Care, she got a pen from her purse, unscrewed the tip of the pen, and pulled out the lottery ticket.

39

CRAZY THINGS

Maggie groaned as she stirred in her bed. Her head was killing her. Is this what it felt like to be dead? She slowly opened her eyes, and even more slowly her vision came into focus. She was in her own bed, in her own room, in her own apartment.

CRAP.

This isn't how it was supposed to be. The news anchors had made it abundantly clear. Heck, everyone was prepping for it. The final curtain. Humanity's last bow. One last push before the chapter ended and the book was closed. It's the end of the world. At least it was supposed to be.

Maggie sat upright in her bed. She looked at her phone. 6:47 a.m. The sun was just peaking over the horizon, spilling light through her partially drawn blinds. It felt like any other winter morning. Except it wasn't supposed to be. That's the only reason why she had behaved the way she did last night. She suddenly flushed with embarrassment and shame, vaguely remembering the events of last night; the drinks, the party, the people. She NEVER in her life had acted out like that. "The end of the world will make you do crazy things, Mags." She chided herself, wondering if – no, desperately hoping that – everyone else at the party was too busy with their own "end of the world celebration" to notice or remember her actions. She fumbled around the blankets looking for the remote control. Finding it, she turned on the t.v., hoping to catch some information on what had actually happened and where they had all gone wrong in their planning. How could the ENTIRE PLANET have been so mistaken?!?

She put on her favorite morning show just in time to hear the anchor saying:

"From the beginning of time, humanity has been predicting the end of the human race and life as we know it. Some predictions have to do with Divine Judgement. Others are about cataclysmic natural disasters. From time to time, alien invasions pop up as the cause of impending doom. Still, in other scenarios humanity itself is the cause behind the coming end of the world. Usually those predictions are accepted by a small band of believers and dismissed by society at large. This time, however, the prediction was so on point that peoples and cultures from around the world accepted it as truth. The signs were all there. So how did we miss it so badly?

40
LIFE AS WE KNOW IT

Good evening. This is the Six O'clock News. As many of you know, for the past few months, Scientists at the National Observatory have been tracking a gigantic asteroid that entered our solar system four months ago and is heading towards Earth. According to their calculations, at the speed it is currently traveling it will reach our atmosphere in two days. As of this moment, they aren't sure what will happen. There's a possibility that it will bounce off, or deflect, and continue past our planet. If it deflects, there should be very little, if any, effect on our weather or life as we know it. But it's also possible that it may enter into our atmosphere.

Now, what they're telling us is that if this should happen, it could burn up as it falls towards the Earth, depending on its structure and mineral content. Or it could remain intact all the way and collide with our planet. If it burns up, it could cause severe disruptions to global weather patterns. It could melt both polar ice caps. There might be storms of unprecedented magnitude. Scientists around the world are speculating that although it may be devasting to people in many places, the planet itself would survive. On the other hand, if it does not burn up and disintegrate, it will strike the Earth with such force that all life as we know it may come to an end. This thing is so large that it could even knock us out of our orbit. And then? God only knows happens next.

Ladies and gentlemen, please do not panic. The president is planning to address the nation in just a few moments, and we would strongly encourage you to stay tuned for his message. Please do not take any action until you have a chance to hear from the president. At this time, we are switching over to our correspondent in Washington for live coverage of the president's speech. Again, let me urge you: do not panic. Please remain calm. Stay tuned. The president is about to begin.

Every television and radio station in the United States used the same script. The media in Canada, Mexico, Europe, South America, Africa, Asia, Australia, and every other place on the planet had similar announcements, and they all ended with the same request: please do not panic. They might as well have told their audiences that in forty-eight hours, they were going to experience first-hand what the Big Bang looked like, sounded like, felt like, smelled like, and tasted like, because international mayhem began immediately. Very few remained calm, and even fewer kept watching to hear what their leader had to say.

People cried. Phone lines were overcrowded, causing lengthy delays. Internet systems crashed. So many people were trying to see their friends and loved ones that massive gridlock prevented them from going more than a mile or two from home. Lovers who had broken off their relationship and wanted to reconnect before the world ended couldn't reach each other. People who were at work couldn't get home. Parents who were out shopping weren't able to get home to be with their children.

Those who expected to survive the huge asteroid headed for the grocery store to stock up on food and water. Those who hadn't been to church in years realized they needed to get right with God before it was too late, and most places of worship decided to keep their doors open for the next two days to encourage and counsel whoever showed up. For many people, frustration turned into anger turned into rage turned into violence.

At nine o'clock in the morning on the last day, the same media spokespersons broadcast this message: *Scientists at the National Observatory made an announcement early this morning. It is their opinion that the asteroid will reach Earth today at 9:15 p.m. Greenwich Mean Time. We believe it will enter the atmosphere. Based on an analysis of it's structure, we do not think it will burn up. We think it will strike the planet and kill all of us. Ladies and gentlemen, we are signing off so that our staff can spend the last few hours with their friends and families. Many emergency services are shutting down and first responders are going home. You are on your own. Earth's history has been a good ride. Good luck and God bless.*

Television and radio stations around the world stopped broadcasting. The world wide web went dark. Telephones became silent. Power grids were shut off. Some people locked themselves inside their homes. Underground shelters were filled to capacity. Millions set out their lawn chairs and waited outside so they could watch the calamity unfold. Wherever they were, people hugged, kissed, made love, sang, prayed, told jokes, laughed, and cried. And at the appointed moment, Earth ceased to exist.

41

THE DEVIL'S PLAYGROUND

The Devil went down to Georgia, he was lookin' for a soul to steal...

That was 45 years ago, and it was a work trip to boot. Nothing relaxing about it. Sure, he got the per diem, but after what Johnny put him through, he actually lost money on that trip. God, how he needed a vacation.

Decade after decade of tempting the faithful, harvesting wicked souls, and causing general mayhem in the lives of humanity can REALLY take its toll on a person. Well, he wasn't a person, but even so – the work was grueling and there was never any thanks for all of his effort. His minions never made an effort to make him feel cared for. Their only motivation was to put in just enough effort not to be sent into oblivion. This new generation was really something else. NOTHING motivated them. Not like the demons of old. Now THEY were some hard-working ghouls! That's it. He would just take that vacation. After all, he deserved it. He could afford to take four days of leave to relax and re-center himself. The office would be fine. Azazel could handle things in his absence. After all, what's the worst that could happen? He leaves and everything goes to Hell?

BWAHAHAHA!

Lucifer laughed at his own joke. It never got old to him. No joke ever got old to him, no matter how many times he told it. In fact, that was one of his favorite tortures at work; telling the same joke over, and over, and over, and over, and over, and.... Eternity was a long time to grate on someone's nerves, and he excelled at it. So, vacation it was. Now to decide where. That was the really hard part. If you think about it, Hell was really the perfect place ever. The weather was just right. Earth had some miserable places, and he had to Goldilocks this vacation and find the spot that was juuuuuust right.

Southwest U.S.A. Nah, it was summer, and place gets hotter than Hell.

Hang out the Canucks in Canada? Nope, even in the summer it can get colder than Hell up there.

Why was Hell always so perfect? Maybe he should just settle for a staycation? Not go anywhere special, just hang out around the house drinking coffee and binge-watching his favorite shows he could never find the time to watch? He was the Lord of the Underworld. How did he not have the ability to make time to watch Season 6? It was supposed to be their best season yet.

That was the answer! He had been everywhere in the universe. There was no place he hadn't seen or visited. After a couple millennia, no place seemed so special anymore. So why not just stay at home, put his phone on Do Not Disturb, and let the lesser demons figure it out? Four days was enough time for him to hit most of the Seven Deadly Sins right from the comfort of his own living room. He smiled as his plan came together. He pulled out his Samsung Galaxy. Ugh, he hated this thing. God was so snooty, keeping the iPhone up there and sending the Android devices down here. Who did He think He was, anyway?!? The nerve! He texted Azazel and Dana, his secretary.

"Going on leave for four days. Keep the fires burning. See you soon." There. It was done. He suddenly felt a sense of peace flood his soul. That felt weird. Obviously, he could never tell anyone about that. Now, time to pour himself a drink, hit the couch, and do nothing at all.

Hell, yeah!

42

EVERY OUNCE OF BEER

"He's a devil!" Jerome screamed at his mother.

"Now, honey, please don't say that about your father."

"But he's mean. He's hardly ever home. And when he is here, he's drunk and abusive."

"He's had a hard life, sweetie. Maybe he'll change."

"Mom, you've been saying that since I was five. I'm sixteen, now, and nothing ever changes! We need to leave."

"I don't want to abandon him. Besides, we have no place to go."

"Then I want to run away. Anywhere but here!"

They'd had this identical conversation too many times.

"Where is Dad, anyway? He's been gone what, four days this time?"

"He said his brother invited him to go on a hunting trip with some friends, and he decided to go."

"Sounds about right. He never has time to do anything with us, but he'll hang out with the guys for four days. Instead of hunting, they're probably drinking the whole time."

They sat in silence while eating their dinner.

"Mom?"

"Yes, Jerome?"

"Do you still love him?"

"Honey, it's complicated."

"It's a simple question, Mom. Do you?"

"Yes."

"Even though he treats you like that?"

"It wasn't always that way, Honey."

While they were at the table, a pickup truck pulled up to the house. Jerome's dad got out, grabbed his duffle bag from the back, and walked toward the house.

"Hey, Jack?" Uncle Randy shouted from behind the wheel.

"Yeah?"

"You want me to come in and be there when you tell your wife and son?"

"No thanks, bro. I got this."

"Okay, man. Let me know if you need me. And tell your family they can call if they want."

"Thanks, Randy. See ya."

Jack walked into the house without saying a word, tossed his bag onto the bedroom floor, came out, headed straight to the fridge, pulled out every bottle and can of beer that was in there, and set them on the counter by the sink.

Bracing for the worst, Ginnie asked, "How was your trip?"

Jack turned around and faced his wife. "Ginnie, we need to talk. But I have to do something, first."

He turned around and poured every ounce of beer down the drain. Then he took the empties out to the recycle bin in the garage, while Ginnie and Jerome sat at the table wondering what was going on.

Jack returned and sat down at the table with his wife and son.

"Listen. Um. Something happened while I was gone. It's like this. I didn't know it, but um, Randy and the guys he hangs out with? They're all Christians, and, well, hanging out with them turned out to be a lot more fun than I expected. Me and a couple guys were talking one night, and they were telling me how they had been alcoholics and abusive before Jesus. And it started getting to me, ya know, and after a while, I realized they were talking about me and the way I've treated you guys. And they could see by the look on my face something was going on inside me. And one of 'em said, *Jack, are you all right?*

So, I told 'em what's been going on here at home. With me at work. Everything. Before you know it, one of 'em asked if they could pray with me and I, um. I said yes. And so they prayed for me, and, um. This is hard to talk about. After they were done, I asked what would it take for me to become a Christian like them so I can be a decent person to my wife and my son, and not do the things I've been doing."

43
THE PERFECT SPOT

Oh, Marty was SO full! They had just finished a veritable feast. To be totally honest, he wasn't sure if this location was going to work for him. He and Jerry, his best friend, had been traveling for a little while look for the perfect place to land and set up shop. It seemed like every time they had a potential location, the giant fangs of life came chomping down to drive them out. It made permanence really tough. But now at last the seemed to have arrived. This was the life! Even when those fangs of life had tried to oust them from this area, they were delightfully out of reach. They were untouchable. Nothing could harm them now! Marty was on cloud nine.

So they had settled down. Marty and Jerry had finally found contentment where they were, fully living in the moment. Every once in a while those fangs would try to dislodge them. Life would claw at them and try to tear them apart, but they managed to hang on through it all. It was hard, sometimes, but it was ultimately a good life for them.

As the days wore on, age started catching up to them. Their appetites waned, but they never stopped drinking in as much as life had to offer. Not every flea is as lucky as they had been, and this Dalmatian had been a real life-saver.

They truly had found the perfect spot.

44

INSEPARABLE

Robert and Sam spent nearly all day every day together. Most people in town said things like, *You two are inseparable*, because, well, it was true. Robert was the man; Sam was the Golden Retriever. Robert was sixty-three; Sam was eight. They went everywhere together. The diner, the library, the church, the orchard, the car repair shop, the grocery store, the ball game, the fishing hole at the creek. And when they were at home, it was still true. The living room, the kitchen, the bathroom, the bedroom, the backyard, the mailbox. *Inseparable*, is what most people said.

So, Sam didn't understand why Robert told him to stay. He didn't know that the neighbor's house was on fire. He wasn't aware of Robert's training in CPR. He had no idea that when Robert went into the burning house, he would save five lives: husband and wife and three children. He didn't understand that Robert died of smoke inhalation.

All he knew for sure was that Robert told him to stay, and being the loyalest best friend Robert ever had, Sam sat in that same spot where Robert had said the word, *Stay*. Listening, watching, smelling, waiting for his best friend to come back.

The neighbors whose lives Robert had saved brought Sam food and water and love. But Sam stayed without moving from that spot for three months. Actually, it was ninety-seven days later when the realtor told the neighbors that the people who bought the place were ready to move in, and the young family whose lives Robert had saved went over to take Sam home with them.

45

YOU NEVER UNDERSTAND

"WHY CAN'T YOU EVER SEE THINGS MY WAY?!? YOU NEVER UNDERSTAND ME!"

The bedroom door slammed with such force that the rest of the house reverberated. Tim sighed. It's not like this was the first time he had heard this from his teenager. It seemed once the boy hit puberty, everything changed. The sweet, loving little boy that was always quick with a smile experienced a metamorphosis and turned into some monster worthy of being a character from an H.G. Wells novel. Honestly, Tim was surprised the door hadn't broke yet.

He really DID try to connect with his son. It felt easier to connect with a 10 year old than this raging beast. He knew the boy; his likes, desires, hopes, and dreams. The beast was indecipherable. The beast didn't like anything. The beast didn't want to be around anyone. The beast simply wanted to exist in its own space without the constraints of parental oversight. That was not something that Tim was ready to let happen. Not as long as the beast lived under his roof and ate his food.

Oh, Lord. Tim suddenly felt like every caricature of an old man who is disgruntled with the youth of today. Is this what he had become? Mere caricature? Principal Skinner from the Simpsons television show flashed into his head saying, "Am I so out of touch? No! It's the children who are wrong." The show proved time and again to be more than entertaining, it was eerily prophetic. Time to call in a pro. Tim dialed his father's phone number.

"Hey, Tim, what's up?" His dad always seemed so cheery.

"It's this grandson of yours. I'm at my wit's end and I'm not sure what do you. His attitude sucks. He yells at the family nearly every day. The door has taken so much physical abuse I may need to replace it when we move. I don't know how to get through to the kid. Where did our loving son go? So, yes, I'm humbly asking for some insight."

"BWAHAHAHAHAHAHAHAHAHAHAHAHAHAHAHAHA HAHAHAHA!" Tim felt like his dad was not going to stop laughing, but eventually he did.

"Dad, what's so funny?"

"You have no memory of our life back in the day?" Tim's father asked incredulously.

"I seriously don't know what you're talking about, Dad."

"You put your mother and me through this EXACT. SAME. THING. I've been waiting for this day to come for so long!

46

IN A DIFFERENT LIGHT

After Freddy's funeral, Molly hosted a small reception at her home. The kids helped by bringing food and setting up extra chairs, just in case anybody came. They were pleasantly surprised when about thirty people showed up to honor Freddy and to offer condolences to the family.

One of the people at the house was a man nobody had seen before, and Molly said to her oldest son, "Max, go and introduce yourself and find out who is."

"Okay, Mom. Be right back."

Max went over to the stranger but didn't come right back because the conversation went in a direction he never expected.

"So, you're Freddy's son, eh. Your dad talked lot about you, Max."

"Who are you, and why are you here?"

"I was a friend of your dad. We go way back. About a year ago, he called and told me about a project he was working on. Then, a week before he died, he called again and said it was just about ready. Next thing I hear is that he's dead. To answer your question, I'm here for two reasons. One, I wanted to pay my respects to my friend. Two, I'd like to know if you or your mom have made a decision about what to do with his work."

110

"I don't mean to disrespect the dead, especially my own father, but his work never amounted to anything."

"I know, but this might be different. Did he talk to you about it? Have you seen it?"

"No. He never talked about it to anyone. And it all happened so fast. I haven't even had the time to look at it."

"Are you still teaching at the university and consulting for the Pentagon?"

"Yes, why? How did you know that?"

"I told you that your dad talked about you. He loved you and was proud of you."

"He never told me that."

"That's like Freddy. Never could talk about emotions. You could be his best friend and not even know it."

"Were you?"

"Was I what?"

"Were you his best friend?" Max clarified.

"I'm not sure, but I sometimes wondered. What do you know about his latest project?"

"Absolutely nothing. Ne never told me about it. But then, we haven't talked the past two years."

"Sorry to hear that. Would you like some advice?"

"Depends on what it is."

"Fair enough. Your dad's workshop was in the basement, I think he told me."

"That's right."

"When all this is over and you have a few minutes, go down there and take a look at what he was working on. He said there was a file cabinet with his notes and sketches. Read it. With your background and expertise, I think you'll appreciate what he has been doing. Here's my card. Call me in a week or two."

The stranger walked out the door and drove away. Max went to find his mother.

"Mom, the guy is the Dean of MIT's School of Engineering and the Chief Innovation and Strategy Officer. Says he and Dad go way back. And he asked me to take a look at Dad's latest project, read through his notes, and then get back to him. Do you know anything about the guy or about what Dad was working on?"

"Not at all. I'm sure Freddy never talked about him. What should we do?"

"There's a lot going on today, but would you mind if I went downstairs tomorrow and snooped around?"

"That'd be fine. It would be nice to have you here a little longer."

It took Max three days to read his father's research notes and examine the device. Then he called the number on the card.

"Hi, this is Max. I talked with you after my dad's funeral."

"Thank you for calling. Are you ready to proceed?"

"Yes. My mother authorized me to speak on her behalf. To be honest, we're in shock. We're filing for a patent and are ready for further guidance."

"Wonderful. I think Freddy would approve."

After receiving the patent, Molly and Max met with their attorney and a representative of General Dynamics. They agreed to sell the rights to Freddy's device and all his research for 16.7 million dollars. After the meeting, Molly and Max went for lunch at the restaurant that had been Freddy's favorite.

"Son, I have a confession to make."

"What's that, Mom?"

Through tears of guilt and shame, she said, "All those years, I disrespected him. It got to the point I thought he was an idiot, a failure, and I hated him."

"Mom, I felt the same way. All of us kids did."

"But now? Now I feel terrible about it."

"Mom, there's no way we could have known this was going to happen. He wasn't there when we needed him. He wasn't there for you or for us kids. He was a terrible husband and father, and the fact that his last invention turned out to be successful doesn't change what he did to us."

"But now," Molly continued. "I see him in a different light."

"I know! He finally put it all together and, well, I don't think I've said this in my entire life . . . I'm proud of my dad."

"Me too, Max. Me too."

47
ABOUT TO EXPLODE

Three hours can be a long time. Three hours can be a short time. When you're at the theater watching your favorite superhero in the newest epic film, three hours passes by very quickly. When you're on the road driving to visit your in-laws for the holidays, three hours is an eternity. It's even worse when your bladder messages your brain and says, "Hey, pal, you may want to find us a place to take a little break."

Pete's bladder sent that message to his brain about 45 minutes ago. Ironically, he had told the kids MULTIPLE times to use the bathroom before getting on the road. He had even made sure he had gone. Most of the trip had been uneventful, but NOW he needed to go? This was so unfair. He hated stopping, especially since they were so close now. 45 minutes more and they would be at Kelly's parents' house.

His bladder rang the doorbell of his brain again.

"YO! ANYBODY HOME?!? I GOTTA GO!"

Even though Pete didn't like it, he knew he needed to take action. He called out to the backseat of the family van, "I gotta stop to use the bathroom. Anyone else need to go?"

"Me!"

"Me, too!"

Well, at least he wasn't alone. Looks like a family pit stop was in order.

"Okay, guys. Next exit with a restaurant or gas station we'll pull over."

But the was no such exit in the following ten miles. Nor was there such an exit for many more miles to come. Pete became a little panicky. He looked in the review mirror and saw his daughters both looked a little panicky as well.

"Just stop on the side of the road," his wife advised. "You can walk a bit into the forest to do your business and I'll help the girls."

"I DIDN'T WANT TO STOP ROADSIDE!" Sam hadn't intended to yell, but the pressure on his bladder turned up the volume on his voice.

"At this point you can stop roadside or spend our vacation cleaning the seat cushions, and you KNOW that smell won't come out easy." His wife was ever the pragmatist. He saw a little turnout on the country road and pull the van over. Then everyone leapt into action.

48
RELIEF

The Psych 101 professor walked into the fifth-floor classroom ten seconds before starting time, tossed her notes onto the podium, looked out at her students, and took a deep breath.

"Today, I'd like us to discuss what people do to relieve stress, pain, worry, or fear. Let's begin by brainstorming. From your reading, your observation of others, and your personal experience, what are some of the ways human beings attempt to find relief? While you're thinking about it, I'd like to show a YouTube video from CBS News about Alka Setzer. Does anyone know the words to their jingle?"

One student raised his hand.

"Go ahead," she said.

"Plop, plop, fizz fizz, oh what a relief it is."

"That's right. Thanks. Let's watch this film about the history of it."[2]

After the video, the teacher continued.

"So, what are some of the ways people try to find relief? Tell you what, for this discussion, don't worry about raising your hand. Just call out your suggestions."

In no time, the students came up with a long list of things people do.

---

[2] https://www.youtube.com/watch?v=icwW6H-PJ-0. Accessed 02/24/2025.

Alcohol, Drugs, Comedy, Music, Running, Talking about it, Reading, Vacation, Food.

Violence, Sex, Prayer, Therapy, Housecleaning, Chocolate, Painkillers, Sleep, TV.

"Great list. Thank you," she said to the class. "Who mentioned Housecleaning?"

A student in the third row raised her hand. "That's what my mom does whenever she's upset. She says it helps her work off some steam and accomplish something before she says something that might make things worse."

"I love it. Thank you. And who mentioned Violence?"

A hand in the back went up.

"My dad's a probation officer. I've heard him say he thinks some of his parolees use violence to relieve their anger because nothing else works. That's what they grew up with and that's all they know."

"Interesting perspective. What about Prayer?"

A student on her left raised his hand.

"Go ahead."

"There's a lot of evidence that prayer and meditation help a lot of people deal with the issues they're facing.

"Yes, that's true. Thanks for telling us about that. And one more, who mentioned Therapy?"

"I did," a guy in the front responded. "Isn't that why we're studying psychology? To learn how to help people find ways to deal with their problems and experience a sense of relief?"

"Good point. Now, if we were to take this conversation in a personal direction, which we're not going to do today, I would ask you to reveal what you yourselves do to find relief. My assumption is that some of you pray. Some of you are using drugs. Some of you are runners. I would guess that in a group this size, every one of those methods is probably in use by someone. So, we have to consider a few other questions. Which of these actions are positive and which are negative? Which are helpful and which are harmful? Do some of these provide short-term relief while other actions bring long-term relief? That's what your next research paper will explore."

A young lady raised her hand.

"Yes, Tamara?"

"What about suicide? Is that possibly an attempt to ease the pain of whatever might be happening in a person's life?"

"For some people, I think it is. What do you think?"

"A friend of mine killed himself. He was unhappy for a long time and wouldn't talk about it. His Mom told me about what happened. I never understood why he would do something like that, but if finding relief from problems or pain is a motivator like you're suggesting, I just wonder if that's what he was trying to do."

"Those are powerful observations, Tamara. Okay, class, if you have any questions as you're doing your research or writing the paper, feel free to email me or make an appointment with my TA. See you next time."

After the last student left the room, she walked over to the window and opened it to get some fresh air. For some reason, thoughts of her son's passing last summer because of cancer weighed heavy on her today. Probably because of the note she found that morning from her husband, saying he was leaving her. He just couldn't handle the pain of losing their son, and wanted to run away.

49

THE BAD GUY

Labels are terrible things. Light vs. Dark. Good vs. Evil. The world is so much more than simple dichotomies. Oh, sure – I'M the bad guy. Says who? These murderers who troll my home and disrupt the natural order of things, that's who! Did I go into their turf and disrupt their way of life? No! Did I go and rip apart families? No!

But people always look for a villain. It's easier to blame the other than to take a hard look in the mirror. So the great white shark becomes the bad guy – something to be hunted and eradicated. If those people on Amity Island had simply stayed where they belong none of this would have happened. THEY HAVE FEET, FOR CRYING OUT LOUD! They don't belong here in my ocean. There I am, an apex predator, just doing what is perfectly natural in the world, and these people have to shake things up. They invade and take over space that shouldn't be theirs. And sharks have to eat, don't we?

Everyone eats. So why judge me for doing what we all do? If they hadn't come into my home, my dinner would have been seafood. I'm only the bad guy because THEY instigated. They invaded. I was only defending my turf. Now everyone blames me and are trying to gaslight others. They try to paint me in a negative light. They even gave me a vicious nickname. Jaws, they call me. Of course I have a jaw. They have jaws. I cannot roll my eyes hard enough at the hypocrisy. If they simply put down their hunting gear and walked away, there would be peace.

Don't see me as the bad guy – I didn't start this war.

50

PIGEONHOLED

Jonathan Worthmore, Hollywood's most famous movie villain, was rich, in demand, and unhappy.

"Why do you grouse and grumble?" his agent scolded. "You have the world by the tail."

"Bill, instead of telling me what to do or think, listen to me for a change," Jonathan retorted. "If money, notoriety, and having steady employment were all that mattered, you'd be right. But there's more to life than that." Jonathan was yelling again.

"What more could there possibly be?" Bill had softened his tone by now.

"Look, when I got into acting as a young, desperate wannabe, I took whatever role they gave me. And I was grateful. But then I got pigeonholed as a bad guy. The last nine movies in a row I've been the villain."

"And what's the matter with that, huh? Nine movies in a row. There are actors who would die to land a role in even one movie."

"Sure, I can be that character. I can be a bad guy."

"You're good at it, Jonathan."

"But I'd rather diversify, have a chance to play a detective, a romantic lead, or even a superhero. I see myself as an actor with the ability to portray a wide range of characters, emotions, relationships, and genres, but all you're getting for me is same o same o."

"How much money did you make last year, the year before that, the past ten years? Huh? Think about that."

"Bill, I'm beginning to think you've become lazy the way you're handling my career and the roles you're lining up."

"Lazy! You're one of the busiest actors in Hollywood."

"So here's the deal. Get busy lining up something different, or I'll get busy lining up a new agent."

"You wouldn't dare!"

"Don't forget, our contract expired eight months ago, and we automatically defaulted to a per-project basis. Say *You wouldn't dare* one more time, and I swear our business relationship is over."

"All right! All right! I'll make some calls."

While they were arguing, Bill's phone rang.

"Good afternoon, this is Bill . . . Hey, great to hear from you . . . He happens to be here now . . . Wait, let me put you on speakerphone . . . Okay, go ahead."

"Jonathan, this is Hugh Jackman. I have a question for you."

"Nice to hear from you. What's up?"

"A few weeks ago, I agreed to take a role in a new action hero series. But something's come up, and I'm not able to do it. I need to let you know that I recommended you for the part. They plan to call you and offer a three-picture deal. What do you think?"

51

A NEW WAY OF THINKING

The meeting was unlike anything in the history of the world. This is not how business was done. Usually, network competitors guarded their show ideas the way Tolkien's dragons guarded gold. No, strike that. Network executives were more ferocious than any monster or demon Tolkien could have dreamed up. They were cutthroat. They were vicious. They were willing to sell out their own mothers if it meant coming up with the next greatest hit that could be milked for ungodly amounts of money. Yet here they all were, in the same room at the same time for the same purpose. They had hit an impasse.

One of the execs from the "Big Four" stood up to address the room. He looked around at his colleagues. He knew how they felt. They were all in panic mode. As his gaze fell on the representatives from some of the smaller cable networks, a microexpression crossed his face. It was hard to see, but people who knew him recognized a look of disgust. The Big Four could hardly tolerate tiny cable networks. They were children trying to sit at the grown-up's table. He sighed wearily.

"No matter your network or net worth, you've all been asked here because you, like the rest of us, share a problem. We have literally run out of ideas for the next reality series. This isn't just a problem with my network, but I've heard the same from multiple networks."

One of the smaller networks piped up. "Thank God! I'm SO relieved! We thought it was just us."

The Big Four exec smiled grimly. "Unfortunately, it's all of us. We've done everything we can think of for a new reality television. We can only repackage the same schtick so many times. As a group of peers, we need to chart a new path for television. Where are we going to go next? What goals should we set? How do we get there? Yes, this is a strategic planning session for the very future of television!"

Another member of the Big Four defiantly raised his voice. "Speak for yourself! Our Island Survival series is 48 seasons strong, and we've held on to the same host for EVERY. SINGLE. SEASON! We're in the planning phase for season 49."

At this every other exec began to grumble to the person beside them. One cable rep shouted out, "Good God, man! Don't you realize that most people are tired of that crap?!? It was novel for the first few seasons. Now it's the same old drivel!" He didn't realize it but he was on his feet, palms on the conference table shouting at the Big Four exec. "We've tried every plausible scenario, and then we've even tried hundreds of implausible scenarios. It's time to recognize that reality tv has had it's time in the sun. Maybe it's time to move on."

The first Big Four executive stood back up. "I tend to agree with my impassioned colleague here. It's time for television to move in a new direction and leave reality tv behind. At least reality tv as we've known it for the last 20 years. We need new vision and a new way of thinking about entertainment programming."

"It needs to have romance!" One of the representatives from some tiny cable channel that only played RomComs spoke up.

"Simmer down, my friend," the Big Four exec said in a friendly tone. "With only seven real plots in storytelling, there will be ample opportunity for romance and every other genre. I'm not talking about plotlines. What I'm envisioning is a radically new way of doing television. Let me share my vision, but we're going to need everyone on board if we're going to be able to pull this off...."

52

DOG BREATH

"Hey, did you hear about the new reality show that starts tonight?"

"I don't think so. What's it called?"

"Something like *Dog Breath*, I think."

"What?"

"Yeah, sounds weird."

"What's the premise?"

"It's like the contestants are dog trainers who bring in their mutts to see which dog is better at detecting whatever it is they're trying to sniff out?"

"You're making this up, right?"

"No, look it up."

Clickety clickety click.

"You're right! It says the producers select a new fragrance or odor each week, and the dogs and their handlers compete to see who's better and more accurate. Sort of a showcase for dog trainers, I guess. Anybody can apply to be on the show to be sniffed by the dogs, and they agree to participate in whatever the theme is."

"Does it say what the first episode is going to be about?"

"Lemme see. Yeah, the first one is where the dogs are supposed to figure out which one of the guests is wearing the most expensive perfume. The dogs start standing up. The losers are told to sit while the winner keeps standing for the next round and they bring in two other sniffers. Last dog standing is the winner. Doesn't say what the future shows will ask them to sniff."

"Sounds like a canine *Price Is Right!*"

"Ha! It does! Let's watch it."

When it was time to watch *Dog Breath*, they grabbed a snack and something to drink and turned on the TV. The first three contestants were a Rottweiler, a Collie, and a Beagle, each of the three on a six-foot-long leash held by their trainer. The curtain opened, revealing three guest participants, each of them sitting on a stool.

"Welcome to the grand opening of *Dog Breath*, America's newest reality show. In this first segment, we asked each of the guests to wear their favorite perfume or cologne and to bring the receipt of purchase. The three dogs will pass by and sniff each person, then return to their starting position. Then we'll ask the dogs to go over and stand in front of the person wearing the highest priced product. These dogs are highly trained. So, without further delay, trainers are you and your dogs ready? Let's give it up for Sheri and her Rottweiler, Tom with his Collie, and Sam with his Beagle!"

The three trainers walked their dogs in front of the people seated on the stools. The dogs sniffed each one and returned to their positions.

"Ladies and gentlemen, let's find out which dog is the best. Trainers, unhook the leash and let the dogs go."

The Rottweiler went right to the stool on the left and stood there staring at the person on the stool. The Collie went to the person in the middle, the one on the right, and then joined the Rottweiler in front of the guest on the left. The Beagle checked out every corner of the stage, behind the curtain, over to the host of the show to sniff his shoes, down the steps, checked out the people in the front row, returned to the stage, and re-sniffed each of the guests, then stood in front of the person on the right. By this time, the studio audience was laughing. Sam was slightly embarrassed and couldn't help but crack a smile, but he knew that's just what Beagles do. The host made a comment to the effect that even the people watching at home were laughing by now.

"Okay, would our three guests show us their receipts?"

The camera zoomed in on guest number one.

"The receipt says $21.99."

The audience applauded.

The camera switched to the center stool.

"This receipt says $47.05."

Again, the people clapped.

The camera switched to the last seat and zoomed in.

"And this one says. Holy Cow! Is this for real? The receipt says $14,199.62. That means the winner of the first showdown is the Beagle! Let's hear it for Sam and his Beagle, Sushi!"

An assistant on each side of the stage held up an APPLAUSE sign and the audience obeyed heartily, including a standing ovation. While Sheri and Tom walked away with their dogs, Sam and Sushi just grinned and basked in their victory.

Two police officers walked onto the stage and arrested guest number three who had the expensive perfume. Turns out that the whole concept for the show was designed to lure the perfume-wearing criminal. Detectives called her *The Perfumed Bandit* because every time she finished the theft of an expensive item, they noticed the scent of perfume, and they hunched that she couldn't resist showcasing her favorite fragrance.

53

A RELATIVELY NORMAL NIGHT?

Parker Landers was in panic mode. He hated puzzles with a passion. He never had the patience to sit and work them out. If he couldn't solve it in the first five minutes, he would throw up his hand and walk away. His girlfriend LOVED puzzles and could sit for hours working on solving puzzles of all types. For Parker, the type of puzzle didn't matter; they were all stupid. Jigsaw, crossword, mechanical/3D…he loathed them all. But today he was wishing he had spent more time learning how to solve them.

The night was supposed to be a relatively normal night – at least he thought it was. He came home from work and jumped in the shower to get ready for date night with his girlfriend, Jessie. He had been looking forward to this night for a long time. He had finally worked up the nerve to ask her to marry him, and tonight was the night. He was supposed to meet Jessie at the restaurant, a new avant-garde place that had just opened a couple weeks ago. He pulled up to the restaurant and handed the valet his keys. The doorman opened the door and ushered Parker inside. That's when things got really weird.

"Welcome to Puzzle House! The maître d' was a little overly enthusiastic for Parker's taste. "Do you have a reservation?" The man's smile was very creepy, but Jessie had been wanting to try this place ever since she heard about it. Time to suck it up and do this for the love of his life.

"Yep, I have a reservation for the romance room." Parker wasn't sure what to expect. With what he had paid, the room better have champagne and chocolate covered strawberries along with their dinner.

"Right this way, sir!" The maître d' walked through another set of doors, and Parker followed without much thought. As soon as he crossed the threshold, the doors slammed behind him and the room swirled as he felt an overpowering sense of vertigo. When his head stopped spinning, he was in a garden with seven-foot high hedges. It suddenly dawned on him what this was. He was in a giant, indoor hedge maze. A disembodied voice from a loudspeaker somewhere out of sight spoke to him.

"WELCOME TO PUZZLE HOUSE! Your exclusive dining experience is waiting for you at the center of the maze. Your guest has already solved the puzzle and is seated. All that's left is for you to make your way to join her. Ready? GO!"

Parker looked around him. The only distinguishing feature of his location was a wooden sign that read, "You are here." Greeeeat," he thought. "The puzzle maker has a stupid sense of humor." He had nothing to lose at this point, so he launched out, picking a path at random as he started to navigate the maze. Five minutes later he rounded a corner and stumbled into a wooden sign that read, "You are here." Ho-ly crap. He had ended up in the same stinkin' place. "Okay, you're a smart guy, Parker," he said to himself in an attempt to pump himself up. "You got this. You just took a wrong turn. Let's go again. Jessie's waiting."

He set out again, this time down a different path. Seven minutes later he found himself staring dumbfoundedly at that ridiculous wooden sign. He took out his cell phone. He needed to text Jessie to let her know he hadn't stood her up, he was just running late because of this insane maze. He looked at his phone. "No service!" He muttered curses under his breath. This was going to be a loooong night.

THE CINQUE TERRE

Mickie's favorite thing to do since she retired from the library was to do jigsaw puzzles. Not just any puzzles, mind you. She loved bright colors, and preferred European scenes. The more difficult the puzzle, the better! And a minimum of 5,000 pieces. Minimum, I tell you! Yes, she was an elite puzzler, a snob, some might say.

"Those measly 1,000 and 1,500 piece puzzles are child's play," she was heard to say more often than anyone could count.

Last Christmas, her ten-year-old granddaughter gave her a 5,000-piecer showing the hillside buildings overlooking the sea in the Cinque Terre, on the coast of Italy. Mickie loved the puzzle but was reluctant to open it and get started because it brought back painful memories of the summer after graduating from high school.

She told her parents and friends that she was going to Italy with a school-sponsored study abroad program. The truth was that she had met a guy, had fallen in love, and had been invited to go with him. Knowing that her parents wouldn't approve and certainly wouldn't have given her the money for the trip, she lied. She and Ron were in Italy, hiking along the cliffs overlooking the water, when he lost his footing, slipped, and fell into the ocean. She never saw him again.

When Mickie got home, she never told anyone about what happened. She was so heartbroken and traumatized that she never told anyone about it. She never told her kids. Never told her husband, Dave, who she'd been married to the past thirty-seven years. Instead, she continued the lie about the study abroad, and made up fanciful stories about the places she had seen.

Granddaughter had never heard of the Cinque Terre because Grandma Mickie had never talked about it. In fact, other than Mickie herself, there wasn't anyone in the entire world who knew what happened on that trip.

"Grandma, aren't you going to do the puzzle?" Granddaughter asked again.

"I don't know, sweetheart."

"Don't you like it? Did I get you the wrong kind? You always finish your puzzles right away, but you haven't even opened this one."

Granddaughter saw the tears in Grandma's eyes, and Grandma saw the tears in her Granddaughter's eyes. They looked at each other, both wondering what to say.

Grampa Dave walked in and saw the two looking into each other's eyes, both on the verge of crying.

"Are you two okay?" he asked. "What's going on?"

Until getting the puzzle from her granddaughter for Christmas, she hadn't felt the old pain or sorrow for a long time. She sometimes wondered whether she should tell Dave about what happened when she was seventeen.

55
PASSION

Long, long ago, long before produce was taken for granted, there was a great meeting. It was around the time when the Great Book recorded: "The land produced vegetation: plants bearing seed according to their kinds and trees bearing fruit with seed in it according to their kinds." The great meeting wasn't planned, not that anyone could remember. The various families of fruit just sort of wound up in the garden. It was an unintentional congregation that would come to be known as "The First Council of Fruit." Many of them were uncomfortable. They weren't even sure who they were – they didn't have any names.

The skinny curved fruit with the yellowish peel spoke up. "Um…does anyone know what we're all doing here?"

The purple clusters of little fruit all tittered excitedly. The spiky fruit with the hard surface and the sharp fronds coming out of his top just bristled. Tensions were running high.

A red fruit on a vine with several others like him spoke up. "Maybe we should all just go home. What are we really doing here?"

"Quiet, you!" commanded an orange, round fruit. "If you don't want to be here, then why don't you just go hang out with the vegetables instead? You may be a fruit technically, but you have forfeited your place with us!" The orange fruit ripped the fruit label off the red fruit on the vine and slapped on a vegetable label.

Everyone gasped. Removing a fruit from the family and forcing them over to vegetables? It was quite an insult.

The Council of Fruit descended into chaos. Everyone was shouting at each other. Then, from out of the noise, a lone voice rose above all the others.

"HEEEEEEEEEYYYYYYYYYYYYYYYY!!!! EVERYONE QUIET DOWN!!"

Every fruit suddenly went silent as this little purple fruit with leathery skin took center stage and addressed the council.

"Listen up! If we keep fighting we're never gonna get anywhere. This is NOT a time to bicker and fight. This is a time to come together. This is a time to get things done! This is how we're going to proceed."

The little purple fruit then when on a naming rampage, organizing and sorting all of his fruitful brethren into different groups.

"You're a banana! You're a grapefruit! You're apples!" On and on he went. The process lasted for hours, as this little fruit stepped up and took charge.

Eventually, the pineapple leaned over to the citron and whispered, "Who is this dude? Who put him in charge of all of us?"

"I don't know," replied the citron, "but he certainly is a passionate little fruit."

56

BEST BIRTHDAY EVER

"Hey, Charlie. Happy birthday, dude!"

"Thanks, Billy. How are you doing?"

"Great, thanks. Hey, I was wondering where you've been all day. I tried callin' this morning to see if you wanted to get together and hang out, you know, celebrate your birthday, but you didn't answer and didn't call back. I tried callin' again around lunch, no answer. What's goin' on? That's not like you."

"That's awful nice of you, Billy, but I had plans, and I was gone early. I got back a few minutes ago and haven't checked messages."

"You never have plans. And it's past midnight."

"Remember me telling you I met someone?"

"Yeah, what's 'er name?"

"Jacquie."

"Oh yeah. You met her what, like, five, six months ago?"

"Well, a few weeks ago we went out and she said she had three questions she wanted to ask me."

"That's weird. Why not just ask the questions?"

"So, I told her, okay, what are the questions? First question was, *What are your passions*? Second question was, *May I plan your birthday*? Third question had to wait til dinner time on my birthday."

"Dude. What did you tell her?"

"I told her I had four main passions: music, basketball, the beach, and Italian food."

"And lemme guess. You told her she could plan your birthday, which is why you couldn't take my call today, right?"

"Right."

"So, what'd you guys do all day?"

"She picked me up at nine this morning, and we drove to the beach. She handed me a gift, and I opened it to see the newest CD from one of my favorite groups. After a great couple hours at the beach, there was this little place called *The Italian Café* where we had lunch. While we're sitting there talking and eating, she hands me an envelope. I open it to find two tickets to the game against the Hawks. I was stunned."

"Dude!"

"So, we went to the arena and saw the game. And then we went to a fancier restaurant than I've ever eaten at. Another Italian place, but a whole lot pricier."

"Did she ever get to that third question?"

"Oh yeah! We ordered dinner and while we're sitting there just chatting, I asked her about the third question."

"And?"

"And she looks me in the eye and says, *Charlie, will you marry me?*"

"No way! What'd you tell 'er?"

"I was shocked at seeing the basketball tickets. You can imagine the even bigger shock when she popped that question."

"Dude! What'd you tell 'er?"

"I told her I had dreamed about marrying her, but was afraid to talk about it because I didn't want to scare her off."

"Dude! Happy birthday! I don't think she's scared!"

57

NICKNAMES

Sean the Warrior.

That had a nice ring to it. Sean had joined the army when he was 19 years old and had seen combat. He personally knew the struggles and hardships of life at war. Coming home to his little village he had envisioned the reception he would receive. He had imagined that the town would dub him "Sean the Warrior" to pay homage to what he had done in service to God and country.

Alas, no one called him that.

Sean the Builder.

It was functional, but it described him and his work. In his village he had helped construct fifteen homes for other villagers. He single-handedly designed and arranged the building of Seamus's shop. He had led the charge to refit the main bridge into the village. His thumbprint was in a lot of the building and architecture of their little village.

But no one called him that.

Sean the Family Man.

He and Maggie had been married for 30 years. They had five children and seven grandchildren. He had been faithful to his wife without fail. Each of their children were healthy, fully functioning adults living on their own with their own families. He was husband, dad, and grandad. The family legacy would carry on and their name would not be forgotten.

Yet no one called him that.

As he walked by the farmer's market, Jennie spied him and flashed him a smile. He was always welcome around town. He was well-liked. Marcus looked up from his produce stand and called out, "Ay, Broim Sean! How are ye, lad?" Sean smiled sadly to himself. Decades ago at his confirmation, when the priest asked him if he was willing to commit himself to living as a follower of Christ, he had the unfortunate chance of having gas and…what do the Yanks call it? Right, he ripped a loud one. In Gaelic, a fart was called broim. The little boys in his confirmation class snickered and started calling him Broim Sean. Fifty-five years later and he had never been able to shake it.

Lord, he hated nicknames.

58

THE EVOLUTION
OF BROTHERLY LOVE

George never called anyone by their real name. Maybe it was because he wasn't confident enough to relate to people in a straight-forward manner, or perhaps he found traditional relationships boring. I don't know. Instead, he instinctively used humor, wit, and his love of language to create a level playing field. He had a passion for words, their definitions, and their sounds, especially alliterations and rhymes, and invariably created a nickname for everyone. Many times, I heard him audibly playing with sounds and words to come up with a suitable name for someone he liked or disliked. It didn't matter.

One of his best friends was a man named Floyd, who he had known for several decades. When they played cards, he started calling him *Filthy Floyd*, which eventually was shortened. By the time I met Floyd, George introduced him to me simply as *Filthy*, as if that was his name.

I made the mistake of telling George one time that when I was a boy, my mother would call me by my first and middle name whenever she was angry with me. *Paul Edward*, she would call out, and I knew I was in trouble. From that moment, George invariably called me *Paul Edward*.

But he couldn't leave it at that. Soon I became *Paul Tedward* because everyone knows that someone named *Edward* was often called *Ted*. But that wasn't enough. No, not for George. Just like *Filthy Floyd* was shortened to *Filthy*, *Paul Tedward* was reduced to *Tedward*. When we got together for drinks or cards, or when we talked on the phone, it was as if *Tedward* had been my lifelong real name.

But he was just getting started. George couldn't stop playing with sounds, nor could he stop messing with people's minds. *Tedward* morphed into *Ted Bird*. But even that wasn't the end of the word play, not if he could rhyme, alliterate, and mess with me all in the same word.

Which means the logical progression—or regression—had to be changing my name once again. So, the next time we got together, he referred to me as *Ted Turd*. And as in the usual evolution of shortening names and nicknames to their final form, until the day he died, my brother simply called me *Turd*.

59

YELLOW SHIRT, YELLOW SUN

"It's not my fault! I couldn't do it because it was a full moon!"

David really looked sincere. Cara always tried to give people the benefit of the doubt. David had certainly never given her any reason to doubt her before. He had always had a lackadaisical attitude, but he had never attempted to provide any kind of excuse like this.

"I'm going to be honest, David. That's a really lame excuse." Cara was never one to pull punches. She prided herself on "telling it like it is" no matter the situation and no matter the person to whom she was speaking. She didn't let it rest there. "In fact, that might be the lamest excuse anyone has ever even TRIED to pull on me! How can you expect me to believe that the full moon was at fault?!?"

David looked like he was fighting back tears. "I'm not being stupid, I really mean it." His voice quivered. He knew what he was thinking, but how could he explain it to Cara without sounding like a nutjob? He took a deep breath to steady his nerves. He blinked away the tears. He had been diagnosed with ADHD and ASD years ago. He knew he didn't think in a linear way like other people did. His brain made connections that no one else ever saw – connections that no one else COULD ever see. He could see a yellow shirt and immediately connect it to the yellow sun which made him think of sunscreen which made him think of the little dog from the

Coppertone ad which made him think of fur which reminded him that he needed to vacuum the living room when he got home.

But he never actually processed it like that. He would simply see a yellow shirt and then think, "I have to vacuum the living room when I get home." Of course, whether or not he actually remembered to vacuum when he got home was a COMPLETELY different issue, but that's how it went. It was never intentional. It was just how his brain was wired. The real difficulty was trying to explain to someone else and bring them along on the journey with him. He slowly exhaled, opened his eyes, and looked directly at Cara.

"Okay, so it's like this . . . ."

60

JUST A HUNCH

"Pssst! Charlene wants us all in the auditorium in fifteen minutes!"

"What? At ten a.m.? Why?"

"She didn't say, but . . ."

"But what?"

"I get the feeling she's tired of people ignoring deadlines, not showing up for meetings, and not getting to the office on time. I think some people are in trouble!"

"What makes you say that?"

"Just a hunch. I have a sense about these kinds of things, and I'm never wrong. You read the email from her yesterday, right?"

"You mean the one asking everyone to cancel all out-of-office appointments today?"

"Yeah. That can only mean something's about to hit the fan!"

A few minutes before ten, all three-hundred-twenty-seven employees filed in and took their seats, a few stragglers coming in late. The boss was up front joking with people, standing next to a funny-looking guy who was having a cordless mic clipped to his lapel.

Charlene had been hired from outside the organization a mere three months ago because the group hadn't met their goals several quarters in a row, and the previous boss had been fired. But everyone thought things had improved. After a brief comment to the funny-looking guy with the mic, she stepped up to the stage.

"Ladies and gentlemen, I know this meeting comes as a surprise, and I know some of you might find it a bit annoying to be called away and distracted from focusing on your work. However, I got a call from higher-ups at Corporate yesterday afternoon with the latest results. I want to congratulate you because in the three months since I have been with you, you all have exceeded expectations. Your productivity is way up. So today, we are celebrating. We brought in a comedian to put on a live show. The funny-looking man stood up and waved. We're providing lunch for everyone, including a sensational live band to perform while we eat. And during lunch, I will personally approach each of you to thank you and give you a bonus. After that, you all get the afternoon off."

The employees broke into spontaneous applause, the band played a catchy tune, and the funny-looking man sprang onto the stage for a surprisingly hilarious routine.

"Just a hunch, eh?"

"Yeah, well, I'm still waiting for the other shoe to drop!"

"Yeah, well, I like our new boss. I think she's the reason things are going so well. And I don't think there is another shoe to drop."

"We'll see."

"Yes, we will."

61
CLOWNING AROUND

This is my life. And people can be SO demanding!
"Make me laugh!"
"Make me smile!"
"Make me feel good!"
Like I'm a wizard that can fix people's lives. I mean, obviously I do what I can. That's the job of a clown. But there's nothing magical about it. I can't fix what's broken in people. But that doesn't change their expectations. There are just some things that weigh so heavy on the soul that a silly guy in face paint and oversized shoes will just not make it right. But the clown tries. We all try.

We honk bicycle horns. We fall over ourselves. We smash whipped cream pies in our faces. We pull out all the stops just to make you forget about your troubles for a short amount of time. And in the end, what do we get for it? We get a crappy paycheck, sticky children grabbing at us, and bodies broken down from years of pratfalls and contorting ourselves to fit into those ridiculous little cars.

Then there are the people who are deathly afraid of us. "Coulrophobia," they call it. I have no idea where it comes from or the technical definition of the word. All I know is that people who have it get SUPER freaked out just by being around me. I don't even have to talk to them. My mere presence sets them off. To be honest, I kinda get a kick out of that. Don't get me wrong, I'm no sadist or nothin' – it's just funny to me how someone who's supposed to bring laughter and humor makes people spaz out. That's just one of those things, I guess. The life of a clown.

But you know what? With the hundreds of people who have seen me, who expect me to entertain them and help them experience humor, no one has EVER asked how I'm doing. It's a one-sided relationship. It's all about what I can provide for them, and all that really matters is how I make them feel at the end of the day. They don't care about what I'm experiencing, what I'm wrestling with, what is going on underneath the makeup. It's like that old song from the 60's: "The Tears of a Clown." I can't remember who sang it. I can't even remember most of the words. I do remember that the clown singing it is really sad underneath it all, and no one notices because of the face he puts on.

62

A DIFFERENT DIRECTION

It was never my plan to do this. In fact, when I was in high school, I was always good at math. I loved numbers and really liked helping people. In my senior year, I needed one more elective, so instead of *Cooking* or *Wood Shop* or *Choir*, I took a business class. The teacher was boring, but a nice guy, and I fell in love. No, not with him, with the idea of being a banker or an accountant or something like that. They made decent money, there was always a job in that line of work, and I could help people in the process. Perfect!

But a few weeks after graduation, my life went a different direction. My parents took me and my little brothers to the circus. My first time ever seeing *The Greatest Show on Earth*! Except when I went to the movies with my boyfriend, and we saw *The Greatest Showman*. Wow! Those people can sing and dance. I can't do either one.

Anyway, there we were, sitting in the bleachers under *The Big Top*. The animals and performers making their grand entrance, music blaring, lions roaring, seals barking, and clowns making everyone laugh.

Suddenly, one of the clowns tripped and fell right in front of us, banging his head on the corner of the bleachers, gashing the side of his head, blood everywhere. There was so much noise that nobody even knew what happened, except those of us sitting right there.

Anyway, without thinking or talking, my dad being a former

Navy Medic, jumped out of his seat and started helping the guy. Also without thinking or talking, I jumped out of my seat and took over the role of the clown. The year before, I wore a clown costume for Halloween and had put the wig in my backpack for this trip to the circus, just for fun.

I picked up the clown's bag of tricks and gags, got into the lineup, and it was at least ten minutes before one of the circus managers realized the usual clown wasn't there. He came up to me. "Hey! What are you doing here? Where's *Jonesy the Clown*?"

I was taught to always tell the truth, so I did.

"Jonesy tripped and split his head open before the show even started. My dad is giving him first aid back in Section 54, front row. I knew the audience expected to see a clown, so I jumped in line, put on my wig, and started clowning around."

"My oh my! You're pretty good! You're hired."

Whatever happened to Jonesy, you ask? Well, he recovered and kept his job. In fact, the circus asked us to be a team, and he taught me so much about the industry. He was only three years older than me. We fell in love and got married. That was thirty years ago next June. I still have the Halloween costume and the wig. And Jonesy's original bag of tricks and gags.

In the off-season, when the performers scattered and everyone recuperated, I took classes. It took me a lot longer than if I went to school full-time, but I gradually got a degree in *Accounting*. This has been *A Ton o' Fun*, as the circus advertisement says. But I think it's time I started doing what I set out to do a long time ago. I lined up a job with an agency in Tampa, and after a two month vacation, I'll finally get to be an accountant. My first client will be *Jonesy*. He runs a school for clowns, now.

ABOUT THE AUTHORS

Christopher is, above all things, a lover of stories! And, while stories captivate our hearts and minds, we still have to live in the real world. In the real world, Christopher is a husband, father of three teenagers, Navy chaplain, and personal coach. He holds multiple graduate degrees in religious studies. He loves connecting with people in life and on social media. You can connect with him on most major platforms @ChaplainLinzey.

Paul Linzey is an award-winning author who completed the Master of Fine Arts in Creative Writing at the University of Tampa with a dual emphasis in Fiction and Nonfiction. He uses his full name for nonfiction (Paul E. Linzey), and his first and middle initials for fiction (P.E. Linzey) as a way of differentiating. You may see his full list of writings at paullinzey.com and message him using the Connect page.